REUNITED

LONNIE C. LARSON

ISBN 978-1-967361-00-7 (Paperback)
ISBN 978-1-967361-01-4(Ebook)

Inquiries and Book Orders should be addressed to:

Leavitt Peak Press
17901 Pioneer Blvd Ste L #298, Artesia, California 90701
Phone #: 2092191548

For Steffanie Sue Larson and Jonathan.

Foreword

…"Your honor," Gheron started, "I would like to speak on Mr. Larson's behalf.

"I consider this an honor, Ambassador Gheron," the Chief Justice said, "Please continue."

"You have before you the creator of the great League of United Planets," Gheron said.

"We all know of your accomplishments Ambassador," the Chief Justice stated.

"I am not referring to myself," Gheron continued, "I was only the instrument through which the League prospered and grew. Sitting in this court today is the true creator of the League. It was his great inspiration that enabled me to start the journey. Without his vision, there would be no League of United Planets. Your honors and distinguished representatives, I give you the founder of the League of United Planets, Mr. Robert J. Larson."

There was a collective gasp and then the room fell silent.

"Impossible Ambassador Gheron, the Chief Justice said, "Everyone here knows that you started the League three hundred years . . . ago . . . Oh, ah please continue."

Chapter One

Bob Larson was enjoying the cool autumn weather of October as he pursued his favorite pastime. Bob was an "amateur" astronomer; but you'd never know it by all the equipment he had. He had built a fully stocked observatory in one of the silos on his farm. He was focused on the planet Jupiter and taking photographs when something crossed his field of view. He grabbed his spotting scope, turned down the magnification and started tracking the object. He could not believe his eyes; 'is that a real UFO,' he asked himself. The object was moving slow so, using his laptops software, he adjusted his main telescope and followed it across the night sky. He took a few pictures and then the object changed direction and seemed to head straight towards Earth. He watched as the object got bigger and bigger on the screen of his laptop, 'how cool is this,' he thought.

Suddenly the object sped up and he watched in disbelief as it darted from side to side. He watched as it neared Earth and entered the upper atmosphere. It looked like a big meteor as fire wrapped around the object when it hit the heavier layers of atmosphere. It was heading right in his direction and he could hear the roar as it tore through the air. It crashed in an open field on his country farm property. He jumped in his old four-wheel drive pickup and drove out to the field. When he arrived at the site of impact he almost fainted, half expecting to see a meteorite instead he was staring at a spacecraft.

The ship was rectangular, about thirty feet long and roughly ten feet high and ten feet wide, it had a large gash in the hull big enough for a man to crawl into. He grabbed his flashlight and a first aid kit and cautiously approached the craft. He made his way into the ship and found himself standing in what looked like the main control area. He saw four alien beings, they looked human, two were still strapped into their seats but two had been thrown onto the floor. He approached one of the two aliens that were on the floor and he realized that he had died from the impact, the other being moaned and when he examined him he realized that he was in pretty bad shape.

Using his first aid training he applied pressure dressings to the aliens wounds and stabilized him. He looked around and then he saw that one of the two aliens that had been strapped in was standing over him, as he backed away the alien held out a hand and motioned for him to come back.

Bob watched as the alien moved some small hand held device over the body of the alien he had been working on and then over the body of the alien that had died. The alien said something to his crew mate and then he retrieved a body bag from a compartment at the rear of the cabin and the two of them placed the dead alien inside it and then placed him in the compartment and sealed the door.

When they approached Bob they scanned him and then they scanned the injured alien again. One of the aliens took out a small round object from a compartment and then held it out for Bob and made a gesture for him to take it. Bob tentatively reached out a hand and the alien placed it in it, Bob was examining the object when one of the aliens spoke again.

"We have to try and send out a distress call Shaan," he said.

"I agree Dahl," he replied.

Bob could now understand the two aliens as they talked and he realized that he was given a translator device and he also learned that the injured alien was their captain.

"Excuse me guys but we have to get you and this ship out of my field," Bob stated.

"Why?" The aliens asked.

"Well, if other people saw your ship crash as I did, they might call the sheriff to report it. If that happened, and they find you here, then the government will get involved and I have a pretty good idea you won't like the results. What I'm going to do will be against my government's laws but I would rather take that risk and help you then have you turned over to them. I have some equipment at my farm that I'm sure will be heavy enough to haul your ship on. I'll be back as soon as I can with the equipment, you be ready," Bob explained and then he jumped in his truck and sped off.

By the time Bob returned with the necessary equipment the two aliens had discussed the situation and agreed to let him help them. It took about an hour to get the ship loaded onto the trailer and strapped down.

"I've got an idea to help throw the law off our trail should they show up," Bob told them. "It's deceptive, but if it works it should buy us some time."

Then Bob took a military rifle out of his truck. The aliens were concerned and Bob told them not to be afraid and that he wasn't going to hurt them. And then he fired several rounds into the woods.

"This will make it look like the military was already here and that there was a situation and then they removed any evidence," Bob explained. "I know you might think this is unethical but it could just save your ass's."

"We understand," one of the aliens said.

When he was finished he helped the two aliens place their injured captain into his vehicle and then he drove them back to the farmyard. With the ship safely hidden in one of Bob's machinery sheds they carried their injured captain inside Bob's home and placed him in one of the spare bedrooms.

Later that night a sheriff deputy stopped by, it was Bob's friend Bill.

"I'm sorry to bother you so late Bob. But we got some reports of a crash or something out this way. Did you see or hear anything earlier tonight? Bill asked.

"Hey Bill," Bob replied. "Yeah, I thought I saw a meteor or something burn across the sky earlier it could of came down close by but I didn't hear a crash. I did hear gunfire about an hour or so later. But I just figured the neighbor was coyote hunting."

"Can I go check it out?" Bill asked.

"Sure, as long as I can I tag along, if you don't mind?" Bob asked. "I'll even drive."

"Well, ok," Bill said.

Bob pulled the Jeep out of the garage and Bill climbed in and they drove out to the pasture. "Maybe it's a small meteorite," Bob said, "How cool would that be? Maybe I could sell it."

"Maybe," Bill said.

When they got to the pasture Bob turned on his spot light and started sweeping the ground.

"Right there," Bill shouted, as he pointed to a burned spot.

Bob stopped the truck about ten feet away from the area that Bill had pointed out. Bill turned on his flashlight and started walking a search pattern at one end of the area. Bob set his spot light to light up the center of the area and started searching the other end of the area. After a few minutes of searching Bob called Bill and said, "Over here, it looks like tire tracks. It looks like someone hauled something away."

Bill studied the tracks and then Bob 'happened' to shine his light on the ground where the shell casings were laying and then Bill shouted, "What's that?"

"What?" Bob asked.

"There, those look like rifle casings," Bill said as he knelt down closer.

"Don't touch them," Bob exclaimed.

"Why not?" Bill asked. "Fingerprints," Bob told him.

"Right," Bill said. "You should've been a cop."

"No thanks," Bob said.

Then Bill used his pen and picked them up and put them in a bag.

"Looks like the military was here already and hauled something away," Bob offered as he planted the seeds of conspiracy in his friend's head.

"Well, it looks like were not gonna find anything more tonight," Bill said. "We might as well get back to the house. I'll have the casings checked for fingerprints in the morning."

They drove back to the house.

"Keep me informed if you could," Bob said as Bill walked over to his squad.

"I'll see what I can do," Bill said as he got in his squad and drove off.

The aliens spent the next few days working on their ship and tending to their injured captain, Bob helped as much as he could by going into town and getting electronic parts and other items for them to try and use on the ship. Finally they were able to get the radio working and they sent out a distress call. All they could do now was wait and hope that it would be answered.

In the meantime the captain had regained consciousness, he told Bob that his name was Gheron. Later he talked with Dahl and Shaan and they informed him of the progress they had made on the ship and also the help that Bob had provided. A few nights later Bob woke up and he saw what looked like bright lights outside. He thought that it might be men from the government coming to search his property. It turned out to be a rescue ship that had intercepted the distress call a few days earlier. When the ship landed four aliens got out, Dahl went out and talked with their captain and then they came to the house. Bob invited them in and they talked for a bit and then they said that it was time to leave.

As they were getting ready Gheron came over and thanked Bob for everything that he had done for them. As Bob handed the translator device back to Gheron he said, "Keep it."

After the goodbyes' were said it was time to go, the rescue ship lifted off and hovered over the damaged ship and some kind of beam came out and when they flew off the damaged ship was pulled along with them.

Chapter Two

A year later Bob was sitting in his home one night when there was a knock at the door. He got up and when he opened the door he saw three strangers standing there. It took him a minute but he soon recognized one of the men as Dahl from the crashed space ship that previous year. He invited them inside and asked them how he could help them.

Dahl spoke, "It has been discussed at great length and Gheron would like to invite you to come to our world, Berillion. Gheron has a surprise in store for you."

"I don't know," Bob started. "I'm not sure I . . ."

"We can assure you sir that you will be well treated and that no harm will come to you," Dahl interrupted.

After some careful deliberation Bob decided to go with them. Bob said that it was late and that they should rest and then leave the next evening.

The next day Bob called Jack, a lawyer friend of his, and told him that he was going to be gone on a business trip for an extended period of time. Then asked him to make sure his farm was taken care of until he returned, Jack agreed to help out. Bob packed a couple of suitcases and spent the rest of the day securing the house and property as if he were going on vacation. He canceled the newspaper, contacted the post office to hold his mail and had the electric company put him on the vacation rate.

When night came he nervously climbed into the alien ship and they took off. Bob couldn't believe what was happening to him. He had to pinch himself several times to make sure he wasn't dreaming.

Bob counted the days and it seemed like it was taking forever to get to the aliens home world but it was only a few weeks, maybe a month. Then Dahl came and got Bob and brought him up to the bridge of the ship.

"Turn on the view screen." Dahl ordered.

When the view screen came on Bob looked up at it and he saw the second most beautiful planet that he had ever seen. It was very similar to Earth. "Welcome to Berillion," Dahl said.

As they made their approach two ships came up from the surface and escorted them down to the planet. After the ship had docked Bob and Dahl were taken to the home of their planets prime leader. It was a huge palatial estate; Bob was given quarters there and allowed to rest. He was told that there would be a banquet in his honor later that evening.

That night Gheron and his family came by and escorted Bob to the banquet, and when Bob saw Gheron's daughter, Leah, it was love at first sight. After they had eaten there was an awards ceremony where Bob was presented with a medal and an award certificate. He was given diplomatic status, and then Bob asked if it would be ok to stay a while and the heads of state told him that it was ok. While there, Bob tried to spend as much time as he could around Gheron's daughter Leah. She was an experienced pilot and a commander in the planetary defense force.

Bob asked if it would be ok to go along on training flights and learn to become a pilot himself. It was granted and he asked that he be assigned to Leah's group. Bob was turning out to be a very skilled pilot and Leah was impressed, she was starting to like this human.

One day, while on a routine practice patrol, Bob found his formation had flown close to a large group of giant space bourn creatures; he was panicked and quickly radioed for instructions. Leah told him not to panic, that these creatures were friendly and were often used as a means of personal transportation. Bob was confused and realized he had a lot to learn if he were going to stick around.

Well it took about six months but Bob finally wore Leah down and when he asked her to marry him she accepted. It was during the next year that Bob learned all about the leviathans that the Berillion's use as space ships. Leah explained how the Berillion's and leviathans communicate telepathically. Leah would take Bob out with her on her leviathan, the Arrgott, whenever she could get free from her duties. It took quite a while and lots of patience but Bob was eventually accepted as the second pilot by Leah's leviathan, Arrgott, she had a distinct personality and it somehow meshed with Bob's own personality. Leah was again impressed because as a rule once a leviathan bonds with a pilot it was rare for them to accept another.

Bob had just gotten back from a two month stay on Earth where he had checked up on his property to make sure everything was still in order, when there was a report that several large alien ships were heading for Berillion. A small group of ships flew out to intercept them and find out their intentions. When there was no response, a second group of ships flew out and reported back that they were under attack.

The planetary defense fleet flew into action, Bob asked to join in but was turned down at first, but Bob persisted and was eventually allowed to help. Leah's group had been assigned to the low orbit protection detail so Bob assisted with transporting supplies to the ships using the Arrgott.

"How ya doin Babe?" Bob asked out loud just as they dodged a laser blast.

'Ok,' Bob heard in his head.

Bob jumped, even though it had been almost a year now, Bob still found it unsettling to hear her voice inside his head.

'Keep your senses sharp Babe, we're not out of the woods yet,' Bob thought.

'You got it,' came the reply in his head.

The battle went on for another day. Many, if not most, of the Berillion ships had been destroyed or disabled.

"Attention all ships," came a voice over the radio, "We are evacuating the planet. All available ships report to docks and prepare to accept passengers."

Bob immediately landed and took on twenty-five passengers and supplies, and then he lifted off. He was with a group of four transport vessels and two fighter escorts. On his view screen he could see thousands of Berillion ships leaving the planet, all heading in different directions at top speed.

Bob's little group of ships had been flying for a week and there was no sign of them being followed. "We need to find a safe port," the pilot of one of the transports said over the radio.

"How many survivors do we have?" One of the fighter pilots asked.

"I've got the count right here," the lead transport pilot said. "We have three thousand and thirty-six passengers and crew, and enough supplies to last six months.

"Hey guys," Bob said. "How about we go to my world? Earth, if we ditch the fighters it will only take six weeks at top speed. Once we get there you can at least gather supplies and make plans from there."

"Why do we need to leave the fighters?" One of the pilots asked.

"Because they can't fly super light speed," answered the pilot from the lead transport.

"They could dock with a couple of the transports and then we can still have the fighters for protection," one of the other transport pilots interjected.

"Sounds like the makings of a plan," Bob said. "Let's do it then. When we get to Earth we'll have to go in under the cover of darkness and land away from any heavily populated areas. Remember, Earth is a lot less advanced than you are. But you are similar enough in appearance that you should blend in without any difficulty."

"What if some of the passengers don't want to spend the rest of their lives on Earth?" The pilot of one of the transports asked.

"Look," Bob said. "I said you can stay long enough to have the ships resupplied and make an exit strategy. Whoever wants to stay and live on Earth can do so. The rest of you can leave for another system."

"That sounds good to me," the lead transport pilot stated. "We can all agree to do that."

"Agreed," came a mutual reply from the rest of the ships pilots.

"Good," Bob said. "As soon as the fighters are secured we hit hyper light to Earth."

Approximately one third of the Berillions decided to stay on Earth. The rest of the group spent the next week restocking the ships for their journey. They evenly distributed themselves between the four transport ships and then they said goodbye and took off for parts unknown.

Chapter Three

Bob had been back on Earth for about six months now. He couldn't sleep and he was lying in his bed thinking about what he was going to do next when there was a knock at the door. Bob looked at the time; it was 6:00am, time to get up anyway. When Bob looked out the window he saw a sheriff's squad parked in the drive. Bob opened the door and it was his friend Bill.

"Hey Bill, What's up?" Bob asked.

"I don't really know how to say this," Bill began, as he scratched his head. "But we have a woman at the office without any ID. She says she is a friend of yours."

"Ok, Give me a minute to get dressed and I'll follow you in to town," Bob said.

When Bob got down to the sheriff's office he saw the woman sitting there and recognized her as one of the Berillions that had decided to stay on Earth. "Abby!" Bob exclaimed. "What are you doing here?"

"I needed to talk to you," she said. "I was wondering if you could do me a favor."

"Sure Abby," Bob said. "Just give me a second to clear this up. Hey Bill, this is a good friend of mine, her name is Abby and we met a few months ago when I was out of town on business. I'll vouch for her."

"Ok then, I knew there had to be a reasonable explanation for all this," Bill said with a wink.

"Right, you got it," Bob answered with a wink of his own.

Bob took Abby to the farm and on the way there she explained, "I want to leave Earth. I miss my family and friends. I was hoping that you could help me find out where the transports went."

"Hmm, that could be a monumental task," Bob said. "We don't know what direction they headed or how far they had to go to find civilization either. What the heck, I'll give it a shot, what have we got to lose anyway but a little time."

Bob had the Arrgott send out a radio call for any information that might be available on the Berillions whereabouts he also called a few of the Berillion refugees and asked them if they could find out anything. While he waited for a reply he and Abby spent the next few days loading supplies onto the Arrgott. Then Bob received a phone call from one of the Berillions living in Texas. He said that one of the ships pilots had talked about going to the planet Deron in the Bernie system. Bob thanked him and told Babe to check her memory and see if she had any information about the Bernie system. She said yes and as soon as she had plotted a course they were off. Babe informed Bob that the trip was going to take about four months.

Bob and Abby kept busy with general house keeping and they each took their turns with the cooking and standing watch. One night a few months into the trip Abby knocked on the door of Bob's cabin. Bob invited her in and asked her what she needed.

"I was wondering," she started. "Do you think I'm pretty?"

Bob was a little shocked but he said, "Sure Abby, I think you look beautiful. I think any Berillion male would love to have you as a mate."

"What about an Earth male?" She asked.

"Why yes, Abby, I believe had you stayed on Earth you could have had your pick of any man there," Bob answered. "Is that why you left? You didn't think anybody liked you?"

"No that's not it," Abby continued. "I really do miss my family. It's just that we have been on this ship for a couple of months now and you haven't asked me in."

Bob was stunned and finally said, "Well Abby, you did know that I am married to Leah? It hasn't even been a year since the evacuation of your home world. I, we, don't even now if she is dead or if she made it off the planet and to safety."

"I know, I'm sorry if I've upset you, I didn't mean to do that," Abby muttered.

"That's ok. Look, I'm not upset. I'm actually flattered that you would even think of me in that way. You are very beautiful and I do love you, just not in that way, at least not right now," Bob replied.

"Oh boy," Abby said. "This is going to make the rest of the trip awkward."

"No it's not," Bob said. "If anything it will be more exciting. You won't have to dance around your feelings anymore. Now you can be yourself and not have to worry about anything."

"That's true, thanks Bob," Abby said.

Before they knew it they were on approach to the planet Deron in the Bernie system. Bob made a call on the radio and he was shocked to learn that ships similar to the ones that attacked Berillion had attacked this planet as well.

Bob asked them if they were all right and they told him that they defeated the attackers. Bob was grateful and he asked them if there were some Berillion refugees on the planet. He was informed that there were about five thousand or so.

"Do you have a list of their names?" Bob asked.

"Yes we do," came the reply.

"Will you send it to me?" Bob asked.

"We will have it ready by the time you reach our planet," Bob was told.

"Thank you," Bob said. "We should be there in about an hour."

"We will be expecting you," came the reply back.

As he parked the Arrgott into a high orbit Bob contacted Deron and asked for coordinates for beam down. He received the coordinates and the list of the Berillion refugees that were scattered about their world. Bob asked Babe to check the list and see if Leah's name was on it. A few minutes later Babe informed Bob that she was not on it. Bob and Abby beamed down to the planet surface and took a transport to the nearest community of refugees.

Abby made contact with an old girlfriend, Kim, and was told that her family was staying on the other side of the planet. Kim told her that one of her brothers didn't make it, that he was killed in the initial attack on Berillion.

Abby was devastated, she and Bob stayed with her friend for a day and then they beamed back up to the Arrgott. On board the Arrgott, Abby asked Bob to come to her cabin, Bob was reluctant but Abby was insistent so he stayed with her while they flew to the other side of the planet. Abby made contact with her family and Bob helped her with her belongings.

While on the planet Bob picked up some equipment and put together a cryogenic sleep chamber and had it installed on the Arrgott. Soon it was time for Bob to go but Abby asked him to stay with her. Bob told her that he couldn't do that and that now that he was this far out he might as well start searching for Leah. Abby said goodbye and Bob beamed back to the Arrgott. Bob asked Babe to check her memory for any system that the Berillions had made contact with in the past and that she should start a search. Babe informed Bob that the next nearest planet was Pogh and it was in the Chevron system and that it was just over a year away. Bob said that this would be a good time to try out the new cryogenic chamber. Bob gave Babe the order to move out, said good night and God speed and then climbed into the chamber and was placed into stasis.

Chapter Four

When Bob opened his eyes and sat up he said, "That was quick. Are we here?"

Babe informed him that it was one year later and that they were entering the Chevron system. 'Wow,' Bob thought.

'I have prepared a meal for you,' Bob heard in his head.

"Thank you Babe," Bob said. "I am a little hungry. I'm going to have to devise some sort of pre Cryo sleep program if I'm going to keep doing this."

Bob showered, put on some fresh clothes, ate and then settled in for the remainder of the flight to the inhabited planet in this system. Babe informed Bob that they were approaching the planet.

"Put it up on the view screen," Bob said. "That looks nice. What's the name of the planet again?"

"It's called Pogh," Babe said.

"Contact the planet and see if they have any Berillion refugees staying there," Bob said.

The planets ambassador welcomed Bob and then told him that there were over five hundred thousand Berillions living amongst them. "Can you send me a list of names?" Bob asked.

"Yes, it will be sent immediately," the ambassador replied.

Babe informed Bob that Leah had been there but it appeared that she had left after only a few months stay. Then she said that there was someone there that he might like to meet. Babe put herself into orbit above the southern hemisphere and then she transported Bob down to the surface. When Bob materialized on the surface he was standing outside a nice looking apartment complex and standing by the door was . . . 'Could it be' . . . Bob thought and then he looked again . . .

"Dahl, is that you?" He asked.

"Yes, Bob it's me," Dahl replied. "There is someone who'd like to see you."

Bob followed Dahl inside and into the elevator. When they got out Dahl took Bob down the hall and into one of the apartments.

"Have a seat, I'll be right back," Dahl said to Bob as he went into the other room. When he returned he had someone with him . . .

"Gheron!" Bob exclaimed as he jumped to his feet. "How are you? Are you ok? I wasn't sure you got out ok. I haven't had any news for a year."

"I'm fine, my friend," Gheron said. "My family got out just fine."

"Have you had any news about Leah?" Bob asked. "I haven't heard a thing."

"She hasn't called me since she left just after we got here," Gheron stated. "She said that she was going to look for you. Where did you go after the order to evacuate?"

"We went to Earth after we were sure we weren't being followed," Bob said.

"We?" Gheron asked. "How many got away with you?"

"Four transports, two fighters and the Arrgott," Bob answered. "A little over three thousand people altogether. But only a third stayed, the rest regrouped and headed for parts unknown. I just came from Deron in the Bernie system, I had to take someone there and we lucked out. She found most of her family there and some friends."

"Hmm, Deron huh," Gheron said. "That's a good planet. We've been friends with them for some time. I'm glad to hear that. So, how have you been?"

"I've been better, Bob answered. "I miss Leah, are you sure you don't know where she might have gotten off to?"

"I haven't got a clue," Gheron said. "She just took off. She didn't say a word as to where she was headed. She just said she was going to look for you."

"Do you think she went to Earth?" Bob asked.

"She could've," Gheron said. "The trip would take over a year from here."

"That means I was already on my way here by the time she would've gotten there," Bob stated.

"It would appear so my friend," Gheron said. "I'm sorry for that. You are welcome to stay here as long as you like. You are my guest and I'm still in your debt."

"Thank you Gheron," Bob said. "I think that I will stay for a while. Maybe Leah will come back here when she finds that I'm not there."

"Good thinking," Gheron said. "In the meantime, I will have the word put out that you are here. Maybe if Leah gets to a planet that's connected she will get the message and return."

"I hope so," Bob said. "I really hope so. It's to bad more systems aren't connected."

Bob stayed with Gheron for a few days until he could find an apartment of his own. He would have the Arrgott listen to the radio chatter to see if she could pick up anything on Leah's whereabouts.

One day Gheron approached Bob and asked to talk. Bob said sure thing and they went into Gheron's library.

"Do you remember when you first arrived you said you wished more systems were connected?" Gheron asked.

"Yes, I remember," Bob said.

"What did you mean by that?" Gheron asked.

"Well, Back on Earth," Bob started. "We have a lot of individual nations and countries sharing the same planet. For the most part we coexist peacefully but there have been more than a few times when some of these countries would forget that we share the same air and start a war with their neighboring countries. One of the early presidents of the United States of America, that's the country I'm from, tried to establish a "League of Nations". He couldn't get the support from the other nations and it sort of died off. Later, there was another big war and it involved many countries, including the United States. After this war, another one of our presidents tried again to establish an organization of the nations. It's because of that war that the leaders of some of these nations decided to agree to a pact to protect each other. Later, as more and more nations grew and developed, they realized that they needed some sort of worldwide congress where delegates from these nations could meet and organize rules as to how to continue to coexist peacefully. We call it the "United Nations" and for better or worse, it does work. Now, if there were some way that the developed systems in this quadrant could come together, unite, so to speak, then they could come to the aid of each other. It might've helped Berillion when the Cyborgs attacked."

"For a culture less advanced then us, you sure can show some intelligence," Gheron stated.

"Yeah," Bob replied. "We do have our moments."

"Yes you do," Gheron said. "I'm sorry to cut our chat short but I have a meeting to attend to. We'll talk again soon.

"Sure," Bob said as he got up, shook Gheron's hand and then left . . .

Bob stayed on Pogh for almost two years and still there was no word from Leah. Bob decided to go back to Earth for a little while, he had been gone for just a little over three years now and he knew it would take another to get to Earth and he was concerned about his farm.

"Well Gheron," Bob started. "I am going to go to Earth for a while. I want to see my daughter and check on my property."

"I understand," Gheron said. "If I should hear from Leah, I'll let her know you were here and tell her where you went."

"Thank you Gheron," Bob said. "I don't know how long I'll be there. Here are the coordinates to where I live and if she hasn't shown up before I leave again, I'll leave some instructions with a friend to give to her."

"I'll see that she gets them if she contacts me," Gheron said. "Safe journey my son."

"Thank you Gheron," Bob said. Then he made his goodbyes' to Gheron and Dahl and then beamed back to the Arrgott and headed home.

Chapter Five

Back on Earth a little over a year now, Bob was out splitting up some firewood for the winter when a sheriff's squad pulled into the drive. It was his friend Bill and he had someone with him.

"Hey Bob," Bill greeted. "How've you been?"

"Fine Bill," Bob answered. "What's up?"

"This here's agent Tom Vance, he's with the FBI," Bill started. "He has some questions he'd like you to answer."

"Come on in from the cold," Bob offered. "I got hot coffee and cake. I don't know what the FBI could need my help with but I'll give it a try."

They went inside and sat down. Bob set the coffee and cake on the table and said, "Fire away Tom."

"We've been noticing that you are gone an awful lot lately," Tom started. "Where have you been?"

"I go all over the place," Bob answered. "I can afford it."

"We know that," Tom said. "What do you do?"

"I visit friends and family mostly," Bob Answered. "Sometimes I go places just to see the sights. There's nothing wrong with that, is there?"

"No," Tom started . . .

"Then what's the problem? Have I broken any laws?" Bob interrupted.

"Not that we're aware of," Tom said. "It's just a bit unusual, that's all. You seemed to start doing an awful lot of "vacationing" not to long after the purported meteorite crash on your property."

"About that. Why don't you ask the boys at area fifty-one about it?" Bob asked.

"What are you talking about?" Tom asked. "What boys?"

"The military, probably Air force," Bob said. "Bill and I went out to the site that night expecting to find a rock but we found tire tracks and shell casings from an M-16 instead. Tell him Bill."

"Yeah, that's right. We found some shell casings," Bill said. "And I sent them to the lab for prints and when I called to check on them I was told that they had sent them to you guys."

"I wasn't aware of this," Tom said. "It sounds a little to pat to me. I think you're hiding something."

"Go ahead and check it out for yourself if you don't believe us," Bob said.

"You can be sure of that Mr. Larson," Tom said as he wrote down spent casings in his notebook, then turning to Bill he said, "You had better not be covering for this guy deputy."

"All right G-man, you got me," Bob said. "Bill and I did find a space ship that night and I got it out in my garage. Bill and I fly around in it on weekends."

"There's no need to get sarcastic Mr. Larson," Tom said. "I'll be checking this out."

"Yeah, why don't you do that?" Bill said. "I've known Bob for a very long time and I trust him."

"Let's hope that trust isn't misplaced," Tom said.

"Well gentlemen, as you can see I'm pretty busy getting ready for winter. I don't have an alien space ship parked in my garage, and as far as you know, I haven't broken any laws. So now, if you'll excuse me, I have a lot of work to do," Bob stated as he got up and escorted Tom to the door.

"We'll be in touch, Mr. Larson," Tom Said.

Bill turned and shrugged his shoulders as if to say sorry to Bob as he climbed into his squad and drove away.

Bob spent the winter on the farm hunting and fishing. He enjoyed doing that and he realized how much he had missed it the past few years being gone. He talked with some of the Berillion refugees whenever he could to see how they were getting on. He also spent some quality time with his daughter as well, now that she was eighteen and moved out of her mother's house.

And mostly, Bob tried to stay off the FBI's radar as much as possible and he would often pump Bill for any information he could get out of him. Bill was a good friend and he was sympathetic towards Bob. Strangely he didn't much like big government either . . .

Bob had invited Bill and a few buddies on an early June fishing trip to Canada for a week. It was something he had once done with his family and it had been many years since he last had been. One evening after a particularly long day of fishing they were enjoying a beer and the campfire when George spotted a shooting star.

"Did you see that?" he shouted. "A shooting star."

"Yeah," Bill said. "That one looked like it was close."

"Naw," Bob said. "Just seems like it. The air is clean and clear up here so everything looks bigger and brighter."

"Oh, so now you are an expert?" Bill asked.

"Not an expert," Bob answered. "It's just that I'm somewhat of an amateur astronomer. It's a hobby of mine and I can tell you when the nights are cool and clear you can see forever."

"I forget," Bill said. "You do have a lot of equipment and a lot of pictures as well."

"How did you get all those pictures of the planets anyway Bob?" George asked.

"Haven't you heard George? Bob's got himself a space ship," Bill replied and then he laughed.

"Well, there's that," Bob stated. "And the fact that I've got a pretty good camera set up and a computer program on my laptop hooked up to one of my bigger telescopes for that sort of stuff. I can take pictures of the stars, planets, nebula and even other galaxies. You should see the shots I got of Uranus, which reminds me, you should see the pictures I've got of your wife there George," Bob joked.

"Ha, ha very funny Bob," George said. "You got a space ship?"

"Yep. It crashed on the farm almost nine years ago. I keep it in my garage at home. I only fly it on Sundays," Bob chided.

"You sure are gullible George," Jack chimed in. Then everyone had a good laugh before they turned in for the night . . .

Back on the farm, a few months later, Bob was mending fences when a black SUV crossed the pasture and headed in his direction.

Bob spotted the government plates and when the driver exited he recognized him as agent Tom Vance of the FBI.

"What can I do for you Tom?" Bob asked and then added. "You realize you're trespassing, right?"

"Sorry, I tried calling but no one answered the phone," Tom said. "I've got a few more questions to ask, if you don't mind?"

"Well, I do mind. I'm trying to keep the neighbor's cattle off my property," Bob explained.

"This shouldn't take long," Tom began. "What do you know about Berillion?"

"Never heard of it," Bob said. "What is it? Some sort of rare metal?"

"No," Tom said. "And I think you know a lot more than you're letting on too."

"You got any proof?" Bob asked.

"Yeah I do this time," Tom said as he walked over to the SUV and pulled open the passenger door. "I got this."

Tom had a young man with him and Bob recognized him as one of the Berillion fighter pilots that had stayed behind.

"Am I supposed to know him?" Bob asked.

"He says his name is Rohn," Tom replied. "And he says he arrived here about six years ago in five space ships . . ."

"How could he be in five space ships?" Bob quickly interrupted.

"He was in one of the five ships filled with aliens and he says that one of them was yours," Tom stated and then added. "And don't be acting so smart."

"Who's acting," Bob said finally having enough. "I don't need to act smart Tom, because I am smart, smarter than you. Do you have a space ship? Huh? Tom. Can you do this?" And with that Bob, Rohn and Tom were transported to the Arrgott.

Tom soon realized that he couldn't move and then Bob took Rohn's arm and pulled him across the room.

"What the hell happened Rohn?" Bob asked.

"I screwed up," Rohn said. "I made the mistake of trusting some woman a few months ago and then this man showed up and started asking me all sorts of questions. He said he knew you and that he knew all about your ship, where you lived. He made it sound like you two were friends."

"Well, he's not my friend. He's a nosy FBI agent trying to make a name for himself," Bob explained. "He was fishing, you bit and now he knows too much. The only question that remains is what are we gonna do about him?"

'I could erase his short term memory,' Babe said telepathically.

'You can do that?' Bob thought.

'Yes I can,' came Babe's response. "Rohn. Do you want to stay here on Earth? Or do you want to go to where Gheron is?" Bob asked.

"What's that? Gheron's alive?" Rohn asked.

"Yes, he's living on Pogh in the Chevron system," Bob replied.

"I will go there then," Rohn said. "Ok then, where are you living?" Bob asked.

"Waterloo Iowa with my girlfriend," Rohn answered and then he gave Bob the coordinates.

"You in love with this girl? And even more important, does she love you enough to leave Earth for you?" Bob asked.

"Yes," Rohn replied. "We were going to be married next month."

"Yeah, but is she willing to leave everything behind including her family and friends for you?" Bob asked.

"I hope so. I'll find out and let you know," Rohn said.

"Ok, you go do that and then you go and collect your things and be back here in a week," Bob said and just like that Rohn disappeared. "Now, about our G-man here." Bob walked over to Tom and asked, "Well, what do you think about my ship Tom?"

"Why can't I move? What happened to Rohn?" Tom asked.

"You're being held in an energy field, and I sent Rohn home to get his belongings. And you didn't answer my question," Bob said.

"Where did you get it?" Tom Asked.

"Nosy to the end huh Tom?" Bob replied. "Well, to be honest I got it from my wife Leah, on her home world of Berillion. It's hers but I'm using it until I can locate her and give it back."

"What are you going to do to me?" Tom asked.

"Well Tom, I'm going to send you back home and you are not going to bother me again," Bob explained as he snapped his finger.

A beam of light came out of the ceiling and engulfed Tom. A few moments later it retracted and Bob and Tom were standing in the pasture once again.

"Where am I?" Tom asked when he recovered and saw Bob. "How did I get back here?"

"You just drove out here. You said you had a few more questions for me," Bob offered.

"I don't remember driving here," Tom muttered.

"Are you feeling alright? You getting enough sleep?" Bob asked. "Maybe the bureau is working you to hard. You look like hell, you could use a vacation."

"Still the same smart ass I see," Tom said. "I'll be back when I remember what it was I was going to ask you."

"Call first, I might not be home," Bob said as Tom drove away.

Bob only had a week to get the farm ready and make all the necessary preparations before Rohn got back with his girlfriend. When Rohn got there he introduced his girlfriend to Bob.

"This is Sara," he said to Bob. "And this is Bob," he said to Sara.

"Good to meet you, Sara. Did Rohn explain the situation to you?" Bob asked.

"Sort of," she said. "Rohn told me that he had to leave the country because he said something to get him in trouble with the Feds."

"It's a little more than that," Bob said. "He has asked to leave the planet and we are leaving as soon as we can. You ok with that?"

"How is that possible?" Sara asked. "I've got a space ship," Bob said. "It belongs to my wife who is of the same race as Rohn. We don't have time to get into all the details, suffice it to say we're leaving in less then an hour and we won't be coming back anytime soon. So Sara, you gotta decide if you want to be with Rohn or stay here and be silent."

Sara thought long and hard for a few minutes. She stared at Rohn and then out at the panorama and then finally she said, "What the hell, I'm in. I don't think I would have been able to keep this big of a secret anyway."

"I love you Sara," Rohn said as he kissed her. "You wont be sorry, I promise."

"Ok then," Bob said. "You got everything you need? We have to leave now."

"I'm good," Sara said. "Let's go." And with that they transported to the ship and headed for Pogh.

Chapter Six

The trip to Pogh didn't seem that long this time with company to share it with, and Bob got to know Rohn and Sara a little better also. Bob told Rohn everything he could about Gheron's escape from Berillion and what to expect once he was down on the planet.

Soon they were in high orbit over Pogh's southern hemisphere. Bob contacted Dahl and told him what to expect and then the three of them beamed down.

Dahl met them in the lobby where he gave Rohn his apartment number and then he said that he and Sara should go and get settled in.

"Say, come on up for a visit before you leave," Dahl said to Bob.

"Oh, so you thought I was going to just do a hit and run?" Bob asked Dahl.

"Well, I didn't know what you had planned," Dahl said.

"I need to talk with Gheron anyway," Bob said.

When Dahl and Bob got to Gheron's apartment he had prepared a lunch.

"Sit," he said. "What brings you back so soon?"

"One of the refugees staying on Earth had a little problem with the federal authorities," Bob answered.

"Nothing serious, I hope?" Gheron asked.

"No," Bob replied. "He just made the mistake of talking to the wrong people. Some FBI agent who has been harassing me for a while took him in for questioning and made him believe he was a friend of mine. I took care of it but I decided it was best if he and his girlfriend came here."

"Are you going back to Earth again?" Gheron asked.

"Not anytime soon," Bob answered.

"I'm glad to hear it," Gheron said.

"So, have you heard anything from Leah yet?" Bob asked.

"So far I haven't had any information," Gheron stated. "I have sent word to over a dozen planets in this sector that we have had dealings with. If Leah had been to any of them they would have contacted me here and so far I haven't heard a word. But that doesn't mean she isn't close because there are over a thousand inhabited planets in this sector alone. Many of them are primitive like Earth . . ."

"Hold on a second," Bob interrupted. "Earth is far from primitive."

"I didn't mean it to sound bad," Gheron said. "What I meant was that they haven't developed into a unified planet yet and that they haven't developed faster than light speed space travel either. Many of these planets are still filled with civil unrest with nations warring with each other. And they still try and subjugate their citizens as well. So if she has gone to one of those planets, she would have to be careful not to give herself away."

"Yeah, that sounds like Earth all right," Bob said.

"Then there are the systems that have developed faster then light speed and all they want to do is conquer and dominate neighboring systems," Gheron added. "Those systems you might want to steer clear of. I'll download all of the information for you and you can give it to Arrgott. You're going to find out that the galaxy is full of wondrous things as well as very deadly things. You are going to need to be prepared but most importantly, you're going to need to be careful. Almost all of the systems in this sector haven't even heard of Earth. A few, like our planet, have been keeping an eye on the Earth and dropping by from time to time to see how you are progressing. That's what I was doing when my ship lost power and I had to try and land there. I thought if I could land safely, I could send out a distress call and be out of there before anyone was the wiser. But our ship was damaged more then we knew and we ended up crashing."

"There are a lot of people on Earth that hoped we weren't alone out here," Bob said. "I'm glad they weren't wrong."

"You'd be surprised at just how many systems there are out here that have taken an interest in Earth," Gheron told Bob. "They are just waiting for the right time to make official contact."

"Thanks Gheron," Bob said. "I appreciate all the information and any help you can give me. I plan to stick around a few more months anyway, pick up a few supplies and then I'm gone."

"It's the least I can do my son," Gheron said. "Stop by and see me before you leave."

"You bet I will," Bob said as he left to go do some shopping. Just as Bob entered the lobby to go out, someone called out to him. He turned to see who it could be but he didn't recognize anyone. And then he saw an alien woman looking right at him and walking towards him.

Bob couldn't take his eyes off of her. She was beautiful; she stood about five and a half feet tall, slender, shapely thighs and breasts. But her most striking feature was her skin tone. She had lavender colored skin and powder blue hair.

"What's the matter?" she asked when she was standing in front of him. "You never seen a Thorian before?"

"No," Bob stated. "Not until just now."

"What? Have you been living under a rock?" She asked.

"Yeah, you could say that," Bob replied. "I'm not from around here."

"I can tell," she said. "Where are you from?"

"A little planet that I like to call home," Bob said.

"Clever," she said as she pressed against him and put her arm around his neck.

"Thanks, you can never be to careful," he said.

"My name is Illia," she said. "And like I said before, I'm from Thoria a planet in the Borjoue system."

"Fair enough," Bob said. "My name is Robert but my friends call me Bob and I'm from Earth a planet in what we refer to as the Sol system."

"Never heard of it," she said.

"That's not surprising," he said. "We're unlisted."

"Ha, ha, that is funny," she said. "I thought we knew most of the systems in this quadrant. Buy me a drink so we can get to know each other better."

"All right," he said as they went out and down the street to a nearby pub.

After several drinks and many questions later, Illia said, "How come you didn't run away in fear when you first saw me if you come from where you say you do? You seem to be taking this all in stride for a race that, until now, thought they were alone in the universe."

"Yeah well, It's a little unnerving," Bob said. "But I have always had an open mind and it didn't hurt that my first contact was with a race that was very kind and benevolent either." They talked for several more minutes and then Bob asked, "So, tell me. What do people do for entertainment around here?"

"It is almost time for the evening meal," she said. "Lets get something to eat and I will show you some sites."

"Sounds good to me," Bob said.

After supper they went to a nightclub for dancing and more drinks. It was getting late and Bob told Illia that he should be getting back to his hotel because he had a busy day coming up.

"I would very much like to spend the evening with you," Illia abruptly stated. This shocked Bob.

"Are you always this shy?" he asked.

"Not when I see something that I want," she replied. "I want you. I find you irresistible and intriguing and I would like to know you better."

"I won't lie to you Illia," Bob responded. "I'm already married to a Berillion. I'm flattered though and to tell the truth, I find you somewhat intriguing as well. There's something about you that makes my knees weak and my heart pound . . ."

"I feel the same way," Illia blurted out. "I want you so badly, I just can't help myself."

Then she grabbed Bob and gave him a kiss. Bob finally gave in to Illia and they headed back to his hotel for the night. The next day Bob walked with Illia back to her apartment complex, talking more as they went along.

"Last night was wonderful," Illia said.

"Thanks," Bob said. "You were wonderful as well and you are very beautiful too."

"I bet you say that to all the women you meet," Illia said.

"No, not all," Bob said. "You're only the second alien species that I have been with since I have left my world."

Then they were standing outside Illia's apartment door and she opened it and said, "You were my first alien."

Bob stood with Illia for a moment then he brushed her cheek with the back of his hand and gave her a very long and passionate kiss goodbye, then he turned and walked away.

The next few days were uneventful, Bob collected the needed supplies and transported them onto the Arrgott and soon it was time to head out. He stopped by Gheron's for a final visit before taking off.

"I have something that I would like you to sign," Gheron told Bob as he handed him a computer pad.

"What is it?" Bob asked. "I'm not buying a set of encyclopedias am I? Because I already have some back home on Earth."

Gheron laughed and then said, "Nothing of the sort. I just want something to remember you by, in case we don't see each other for a while. That's all."

"Sure thing pop," Bob said. "But I'm pretty sure I will be around again sometime."

"I hope so," Gheron said. Then he gave Bob a hug and kissed his cheek and bid him a safe trip.

Then Bob shook Dahl's hand, said farewell and beamed up to the Arrgott and headed off into uncharted territories, well at least for him they were uncharted.

Chapter Seven

When Bob came out of Cryo-sleep he was groggy and he asked Babe how long he had been asleep. She informed him that it had been about one hundred years.

"Let's not do that again!" Bob exclaimed. "That was a bit to much. Where are we?"

'We are nearing the Tiberian system,' she told him. 'I need to refuel or eat as you put it.'

"What do you need?" Bob asked.

'We passed a plasma cloud a few million kilometers out and it is filled with neutrino particles, a food source for me,' Babe said with her thoughts. 'I have to drop you and your equipment off in order to feed. The planet in this system is able to support life and you will be safe while I feed.'

"Well, ok, if you are sure I will be safe then that is good enough for me. What's the name of the planet?" Bob asked as they got closer.

Babe told him it was called Borax and then Babe transported all of the equipment to a cave on the planets surface, said she'll be back and took off to feed.

Bob took the opportunity to look around. This was only the fifth planet he had been on including Earth and he was surprised at just how Earth like it was; heck, he was surprised just how Earth like they all had been.

It had plants, trees, solid ground, water, small mammals and (smack) annoying insects. A few hours later Babe returned and called out to Bob and told him that she was ready to pick him up and then they were off again.

"I have a question for you Babe," Bob said. "Do you know if all the planets in your memory are similar to one another?"

'What do you mean?' Babe asked.

"Ok, so far I have seen four planets now other than Earth. They appear to be very much the same. Roughly the same size, gravity, atmosphere and filled with similar mammals and insects," Bob stated. "So how do the rest compare?"

'Well, I would say that most all of the planets in my memory are the same. It would seem in order for a planet to support life it needs to be approximately this far away from its sun and approximately the same size with proper amounts of liquid water and atmosphere,' Babe told Bob.

"Sounds about Right," Bob said.

'You would know this how?' Babe thought.

"Well, the scientist back on Earth have pretty much all came to the same conclusion," Bob explained. "I'm glad to see that we are smart enough to have at least figured that much out. Well Babe, where to next?"

'There is a system a few months from here we should visit,' Babe reported.

"Ok, you're the boss," Bob said.

'Always,' came Babe's reply. And with that they were off . . .

Bob would spend the next one hundred and fifty years in and out of Cryo sleep, visiting countless worlds and often seeing breath-taking sights along the way.

But one event would stay with him forever. He had come out of Cryo sleep near the Dago system; Babe informed him that they were close to the border of another sector and the nearby planet was a sort of a gathering place for different races.

Bob asked babe what it was called and she told him it was Cantoo. When they were in orbit over the main land mass Bob transported down to the surface, and when he looked around he laughed. What he saw reminded him of an old truck stop back on Earth but instead of trucks parked in the lot, there were space ships of all shapes and sizes parked there.

Bob walked into the building, it reminded him of an old Mexican Cantina. There were aliens of all shapes and sizes, many bristling with weapons, suddenly Bob felt sorely underdressed.

Bob found an empty chair and sat down. Babe had provided him with local currency so when the "waitress" came over he ordered what Babe told him to order before beaming down.

While Bob was enjoying his drink this big mean looking alien came up to him and started to pick a fight. Bob could tell that he was drunk so he said he didn't want any trouble. The big alien got mad and took a swing at Bob, but he ducked and knocked him down. Then the alien's buddy caught Bob from behind and knocked him across the bar.

Bob was dazed but only for a second and when the alien attacked again he was ready. It took only a few minutes and then Bob had both of the aliens subdued and their weapons.

Bob was sitting in front of them when they came too. "Like I said before. I'm not looking for a fight but I will end one. How's this thingy work?" he asked as he pointed the weapon at one of the aliens head.

"Stop," the alien said. "The weapon is set to destroy. We were only having fun."

"Some fun," Bob said. "I could have killed you both."

Then the big guy starts laughing and said, "That is what makes it fun. I am Ktaal, this is Chan."

"My name is Robert but you can call me Bob," he said.

"What planet are you from," Ktaal asked.

"Earth," Bob replied.

"We are from the Planet Warlon," Ktaal stated. "We have heard of Earth and of the puny humans that inhabit it."

"Maybe not so puny," Bob said. "I beat you!"

"Aagh, we are drunk," Ktaal laughed. "I will order us more drinks."

Bob spent most of the night talking and drinking with his new-found Warlon friends. The next day they told him that they had to return to their home world. Bob asked if he could go along and they told him yeah if he could keep up. Then they contacted their ship and disappeared. Bob transported up to the Arrgott and instructed Babe to follow them.

In a few weeks they entered the Warlon system and soon they were orbiting the home world of Warlon. Bob was introduced to their leaders and they were told to leave him alone because he had proven his worth in battle. Many, if not all, of the Warlons were skeptical of this human.

Bob was there for about a week when news came in that the Andromidans had attacked an outpost on Getz. Five battle ships took off and Bob tagged along. When they got there they saw five Andromidan warships blasting away at the outpost. They quickly turned their attention on the Warlon battleships and the Arrgott. The Warlons and Bob destroyed three of the Andromidan ships before two escaped.

Bob transported down to the surface to help with survivors and round up Andromidan soldiers that had been left behind in the escape. Ktaal was checking out a dwelling when an Andromidan aimed his blaster at him. Seeing this, Bob jumped, yelled and then pushed Ktaal out of the way just as the Andromidan fired, catching Bob in the shoulder.

Ktaal turned and destroyed the Andromidan and then turned to Bob to check out his injuries.

"Why did you do that?" Ktaal asked him.

"Because I like you," Bob said as he winced in pain. "That's gonna leave a mark. Are you ok Ktaal?"

"I am fine but you will need medical treatment," Ktaal stated as he ordered them beamed up to his ship. Bob was taken to the infirmary as the ships headed back to Warlon.

In a couple weeks Bob was healed enough to go out and he was brought before the emperor and the High Council. Ktaal and Chan were there as well.

"Who brings this human to Warlon?" The Emperor asked.

"I do!" Ktaal stated as he stepped forward and knelt in front of the Emperor.

"Rise, do you swear that the testimony you have given is true and correct?" He asked.

"I do," Ktaal answered.

"Human step forward," the Emperor barked.

Bob stepped forward and, following Ktaal's lead, he knelt down as well.

"Rise human," the Emperor said. "It has been testified that you nearly gave your life for a Warlon. Is this true?"

"Yes it is," Bob said. "I took a pistol blast that was meant for Ktaal."

"Earth human, you honor us by your actions," the Emperor said. "There has been much talk spreading through our Empire about peace and cooperation but very little action to back it up until now."

"Peaceful co-existence is good," Bob offered.

"Some day perhaps," the Emperor stated. "For now it is my honor to present to you the Warlon Medal of Honor. Wear it with pride, you have earned it. The story of your battle will be recorded forever in our history. Your likeness will be placed on the Wall of Warriors for all to see. Know this, all who stand here this day, this Earth human is now a Warlon Warrior."

Everyone in the Great Hall started cheering. Bob was escorted out and there was a great feast and drinking for two days. Everyone wanted to meet Bob so he stayed there for a few more weeks. Soon it was time to leave so he located Ktaal and told him that he had to go and continue his search for Leah.

Ktaal grabbed Bob in a big Warlon hug and said, "I am your brother. I owe you my life. It is my honor to call you my friend and I will never forget what you have done for me." And then Ktaal gave Bob his battle knife.

"Thank you Ktaal," Bob said as he accepted Ktaal's gift and friendship. "I will never forget you either my friend."

Bob finished his goodbyes and then it was time for him to leave. He beamed up to the Arrgott bid farewell to Warlon, climbed inside the Cryo chamber and drifted off to sleep . . .

Chapter Eight

When Bob came out of Cryo sleep Babe informed him that he has been sleeping for fifty years.

"Ok, where are we now?" Bob asked. Babe informed him that they were between systems right now and before Bob had a chance to ask, she told him that she had detected another Berillion bio sign.

"Where?" Bob asked excitedly.

'Scanning now,' Babe said. 'Got it, setting course to intercept now.'

"How long?" Bob asked.

'Two hours,' she replied.

"Good," Bob stated. "I'm gonna get cleaned up and change cloths and grab something to eat. keep me informed Babe."

Bob went to his cabin and prepared while Babe changed direction and took off . . .

Leah was sitting in the recreation lounge on board the Duncan staring out the window in deep thought when the ships counselor, Meg Wauld, entered.

Meg strolled over to Leah and asked, "A penny for your thoughts?"

Leah jumped and said, "You startled me Meg, what is it you said?"

"It was nothing," Meg replied. "You look troubled, what's wrong?"

"I'm not sure," Leah, responded. "Something is out there, I can feel it. I don't know what it is, but I'm sure it's something. I need to speak to the captain."

Meg looked concerned as Leah got up and left the lounge in route to the bridge to speak to captain Pierce.

Meanwhile up on the bridge, Lt. Braag called out, "Long range sensors have just picked up an unidentified vessel heading on an intercept course with the Duncan captain."

"Shields up, red alert," commander Reese barked out.

"Mr. Droid report," captain Pierce ordered.

"Sir, sensors indicate one ship. Unknown origin. I am not detecting any weapons activity sir," Lt. commander Droid replied.

"On screen Mr. Droid," the captain ordered.

"On screen now sir," Lt. commander Droid replied.

"Magnify," the captain ordered.

"Magnification ten sir," Lt. commander Droid replied.

Bob's ship appeared on the view screen.

"How long to intercept?" The captain asked.

"One hour twenty-seven minutes and forty-one seconds at present speed sir," Lt. commander Droid replied.

"Slow to light speed three," the captain ordered.

"Aye sir, light speed three. Sir the alien ship has just increased its speed. Time now to intercept is ten minutes and eighteen seconds," Lt. commander Droid reported.

"Very well, keep scanning, keep me informed and I want you to check with the ships library, to find out what kind of ship that is and where it is from," the captain ordered. "I'll be in my ready room; you have the con commander Reese, contact me as soon as you have anything."

"Aye sir," commander Reese responded as the captain rose and moved to the door and exited the bridge.

Just as the captain sat down at his desk the door chime sounded. "Come in," the captain said. The door opened and Leah walked in and sat down. Pierce is somewhat puzzled by her arrival and asked, "What can I do for you Leah?"

"Is everything all right up here?" Leah asked.

"Well," the captain started. "How did you know something happened?"

"Just a feeling," Leah said. "Now what is going on?"

"Our long range sensors have detected a ship on an intercept course with the Duncan and we have been unable to determine its identity. Why? What do you know?" Captain Pierce asked.

"Nothing really captain, it's like I said, it's just a feeling I have that's all," Leah said. Just then the intercom came on, and commander Reese requested that the captain return to the bridge.

Pierce and Leah both got up and exited onto the bridge . . .

'We are here Bob,' Babe said.

"Good," he said. "What are they doing?"

'Nothing,' she said . . .

"Captain. The alien ship is just off our starboard beam matching our course and speed," commander Reese reported as the captain entered. "Distance is ten thousand feet out."

"On screen Mr. Driod. Lt. Braag, open hailing frequencies," the captain ordered.

"On screen," Driod states.

"No response sir," Lt. Braag replied. Just as Bob's ship appeared back up on the screen Leah screamed and collapsed to the floor.

"Medical emergency Dr. Balow to the bridge," the captain barked as he knelt over Leah to check to see if she was all right.

The turbo lift doors opened and Dr. Balow and two aids stepped out.

"What happened?" The doctor asked.

"I don't know she just fainted," the captain replied.

Dr. Balow gave Leah a medical scan then gave her an injection. Leah responded and came around.

"What just happened?" Leah asked weakly.

"We don't know, but I was hoping you could tell us," the captain stated.

"I'm not sure, but I think I recognized that ship out there," Leah offered.

The captain asked Leah to explain and she told him that she hadn't seen a ship of that kind in a very long time, and that it resembled the type of ships her people used a long time ago . . .

"What's happening now?" Bob asked.

'I am scanning the interior now,' Babe said. 'No weapons activity just shields.'

"Call them," Bob said . . .

The captain was somewhat satisfied with Leah's response and then he told her to go to sickbay with Dr. Balow for a checkup. Dr. Balow and her team left the bridge with Leah.

"Captain, we are now being hailed by the alien vessel," Lt. Braag reported.

"On screen," ordered the captain.

"Sir the transmission is audio only," Lt. Braag, stated.

"Very well," the captain said. "Open the channel Mr. Braag."

"Channel open sir," Lt. Braag replied.

"This is captain Jonathan W. Pierce of the U.S.S. Duncan speaking how can we help you?" Pierce asked.

"This is captain Robert J. Larson from the ship Arrgott," Bob's voice from the speaker responded. "I'm sorry to keep you in the dark like this but I have to be sure of your intentions. Would you tell me what star system you are from?"

"This is a League of United Planets vessel, and we are from the planet Earth," replied captain Pierce. There was silence for a few seconds and captain Pierce asked, "Are you still there captain Larson?"

"Yes, yes I am," Bob replied.

"Good. I am curious captain Larson," Pierce continued. "We have no record of that type of ship in our data base. Can you tell me more about it and maybe a little bit more about yourself?"

"My story is long and may be somewhat difficult to explain over the radio," Bob said. "Perhaps if you will allow me to come over to the Duncan I could tell it to you in person."

"Sir. I strongly object," Lt. Braag interjected. "We know nothing about him or his ship or what his intentions might be."

Captain Pierce noted Lt. Braag's concerns but gave his permission to captain Larson to come on board anyway. Captain Pierce gave the bridge to Lt. commander Droid as he; commander Reese and Lt. Braag stepped into the turbo lift to go down to transporter room three.

When the three of them entered the transporter room the captain asked the ensign on duty if she was ready to transport captain Larson over. She informed him that she had the coordinates and was ready to energize on his command. Captain Pierce contacted Bob and asked him if he was ready to beam over.

"Ready," Bob answered.

"Energize," the captain ordered. Almost instantly Bob materialized on the pad. Captain Pierce spoke first, "Welcome to the U.S.S. Duncan I am captain Jonathan Pierce, this is my first officer commander Tom Reese and this is our chief security officer Lt. Braag."

"You are a Warlon, right?" Bob asked Lt. Braag after being introduced to him.

"Yes I am" Lt. Braag responded . . .

Then captain Pierce interrupted and suggested they go to the conference room where they could be more comfortable to talk. All four men left the transporter room and entered the turbo lift at the end of the corridor. The doors closed and captain Pierce said, "Deck three."

The turbo lift moved and when it stopped the doors opened and they all walked down the corridor towards the conference room. When they entered the conference room councilor Wauld was already seated there. Captain Pierce introduced captain Larson to her. After they were all seated, captain Pierce asked captain Larson to begin.

"My full name is Robert John Larson," Bob started. "I was born on Earth on June sixth nineteen fifty—nine . . ."

"Impossible!" exclaimed commander Reese. "That would make you over three hundred years old. I find that just a little hard to believe."

"Chronologically speaking, yes, but physically I am about forty-five years old," Bob stated. "I spend most of my time in a cryogenic sleep chamber, with my body in a state of suspended animation and that is why I do not appear to age physically. As a general rule, I would try to spend about fifty years at a time sleeping but I had gone as long as one hundred years once. Never again, to hard on me."

"That's very interesting," captain Pierce interrupted. "But you said you were from the late twentieth century on Earth and as I recall

Earth did not posses this kind of technology back then. So you can see our point if we fail to believe your story straight away Mr. Larson."

"Yes I can see your point," Bob continued. "Let me try to explain. It was in October of nineteen ninety-three and I was looking at the planet Jupiter through my telescope when I suddenly spotted a U.F.O. cross my field of view. I watched this object as it approached Earth and I noticed it was moving rather strangely and then I watched as it came down. It crashed near my farm in the country and I quickly drove over to where it had come down and I was shocked by what I saw. I saw a small craft with what looked like a six-foot long hole or gash in its side. I grabbed my first aid gear and crawled inside. I found that one of the aliens had died as a result of the crash but there were three more. One of the aliens was in pretty bad shape and the other two were not injured as bad. So I concentrated all my efforts on the more seriously injured one. I was able to stabilize him and stop most of the bleeding. I was concentrating my care on this alien so intensely that I did not notice it when the other two aliens woke up. When they came over to examine my handy work they startled me. One of the aliens had some sort of electronic device that he passed over the one that I had been helping. Then they went over to the dead one, scanned him and placed him in some sort of body bag and then put him in a compartment in the back of the ship. When he came back over towards me he had a small disk shaped object in his hand, which he held out for me to take. I was looking at this object and the alien gestured for me to take it so I did. You could imagine my surprise when the beings spoke again I could understand perfectly everything they said. That's when I realized the object was some sort of translator device. He told me his name was Dahl and that he was second in command and the captain's name was Gheron, he was the injured one, the other crewman was named Shaan and the dead one was called Ohman. I sat there and watched as the two aliens looked over the damaged systems and tried to send out a distress call. Then I told them that we had to get them and the ship out of here because someone else may have seen the crash too. I didn't want the law to show up and then have them call in the military. People didn't trust the government with things of this nature back then, so I told them that I would be back shortly. I went back to my home and returned with a vehicle, trailer and equipment capable of loading and transporting the craft and its occupants back to my house. When we arrived at the house I put the craft in a large storage building. I knew I could get in trouble if the government found out but I figured the chance was worth the risk. With the help of the other two aliens we brought the injured being into my house where it would be easier to care for him. Then I tried to help the other two as much as I could with the repairs to their ship. It took a few days to get the ships radio to work and then they were able to send out a message. In the mean time Gheron had finally woken up. As he talked with the others I could tell he was more than just their captain and that he was well respected. A few weeks later, lights and noises from outside awakened me. I thought at first it might be men from the government coming to search my farm but it was not. It turned out to be a rescue party that had received the distress call. There were about four of them and they came inside and the other two beings came downstairs and said it was time for them to leave. They went up to help with Gheron and before he left he thanked me for all that I had done for them and he let me keep the translator device, then they hooked on to the disabled ship with some kind of beam and lifted off and headed back to their home world."

"That's all fascinating," captain Pierce said. "But how did you come to be out here? Now?"

"Well," Bob continued. "It turned out that Gheron was a great leader back on his home world and about one year later I was visited by three beings from their planet. I recognized one of them as Dahl, from when I had helped them the year before, and he asked me if I would come back to their home world with him to be recognized and honored. I was more then a little worried but he assured me that I would be all right. We left that next evening, after I had made some arrangements to secure my residence and property holdings and pack a few things into a couple of suitcases. The trip took about thirty days as far as I could tell. As we approached the planet I was escorted up to the bridge and, there, on the view screen I saw a planet as equally as beautiful as Earth. When we landed I was escorted to a large palatial building and set up in a large room, I was being treated like I was some kind of royalty. They had this large banquet; and afterwards there was a big ceremony where I was presented with a medal and an award. That is where I met Gheron's daughter, Leah. Let me tell you it was love at first sight. It took me a while but I finally got her to marry me."

"What was that?" Captain Pierce asked. "Did you say Leah?"

"Yes, that's my wife's name," Bob said. "Why? Do you know her?"

"It is unimportant," captain Pierce said. "Please continue."

"Right," Bob said. "Well I ended up staying there about a year and a half and then one day, word came in that an unidentified vessel was entering their system. They tried contacting it but received no response, so they sent out a small contingency of ships to intercept it. When they failed to report back in, efforts were doubled to make contact but no reply was heard. Suddenly and unexpectedly the planet came under attack. The defense fleet was dispatched and all available personnel were placed into service. Leah was a squadron leader so she had to go as well. I had been allowed to do some flight training with her squad so I asked if I could help. They didn't want me to get involved because I was only a guest and not of their world. I protested very strongly and they finally allowed me to join them. I took command of the Arrgott transporting supplies to the fighting ships. They gave them one hell of a fight, but the alien attackers were too much for the fleet. So to save what they could, the order was given to evacuate the planet. The fleet was ordered to disperse in all directions at full speed to avoid capture. The battle nearly destroyed the planet completely and out of ten billion people only about one hundred million were able to escape to safety. What a costly tragedy, the Berillions defenses were no match for these cybernetic creatures."

"You fought against the Cyborg?" Captain Pierce asked.

"Yes, that is what they called themselves when they attacked the planet," Bob replied. "Have you heard of them too?"

"Yes we have," replied the captain. "We too have fought against the Cyborg we suffered heavy losses but we were finally able to destroy a couple of their ships, but please continue."

"Yes, of course," Bob said. "After we escaped and I was sure we were not being followed, I suggested we go to Earth to regroup and assess our situation. As we flew to Earth, I instructed my ship to start searching for Leah's bio readings . . ."

"Wait a minute, you what?" commander Reese interrupted. "You 'told' your ship? Don't you mean your crew?"

"No," Bob said. "I told the ship. You see a Berillion's ship is a living creature, a leviathan, it is symbiotic to its pilot on board. The Berillions communicate telepathically with them so in a sense, no orders or instructions need to be given verbally. It took me a long time on Berillion to learn to do this but the ship was patient and now I don't even have to think about doing it. It has become second nature to me, I think about a command and the ship responds instinctively. For the past three hundred or so years I have been searching for my wife and this time when I came out of Cryo-sleep the ship informed me that she had once again detected a female Berillions bio signs. After a long and thorough scan of this sector, we located your ship and set course to intercept. Now for the million dollar question, do you have a Berillion female on board the Duncan?"

"Yes we do," answered the captain. "She has been on board for several years now." Just then the intercom came on and Lt. commander Droid requested that the captain return to the bridge.

Captain pierce excused himself and told commander Reese and Lt. Braag to see to captain Larson's needs for the time being and then he left. When captain Pierce got to the bridge Lt. commander Droid informed him that Leah had transported over to the Arrgott. Captain Pierce immediately called for commander Reese to report back to the bridge as well; when he arrived the captain told him what had happened. Commander Reese was puzzled as to why Leah would do that and that's when the captain told commander Reese to bring captain Larson to the bridge. Commander Reese asked the ships computer to locate Lt. Braag and captain Larson. He was informed that they were in the ships lounge. Commander Reese left the bridge and headed for the lounge.

Chapter Nine

Lt. Braag and Bob were sitting at a table in the ship's lounge talking when Lt. Braag asked him when he had met with other Warlons.

"While I was searching for my wife, I chanced to meet with some Warlon warriors in a cantina on an alien planet called Cantoo about fifty years ago," Bob started. "They were loud and boastful. They spotted me and I think they intended to do me in because they got up and started yelling insults. I wasn't in the mood for a fight and I told them so. Well, that made them even madder, one of them tried to attack me but they were drunk and I was not. I was able to subdue the first one when the other one caught me from behind and knocked me across the bar. I quickly regained my composure and when he came in for his second attack I was ready and subdued him too. When they came too, I had their weapons and again explained to them that I did not want any trouble, they started to laugh and then they ordered me a drink. I spent some time with them on that planet and we became friends. When it was time for them to leave I asked them if it would be ok for me to come to their planet and they allowed me to follow them. They told their leader that I had become their friend and I was allowed to stay. I was on the planet for a couple of weeks when word came in about an attack on one of their outposts by the Andromidans. A war party left for the outpost on Getz and I went with them. When we arrived we fought and took out three of the Andromidan warships, two managed to escape. I was down on the planets surface, to help with survivors when we were jumped by a few Andromidans that were left behind, I was injured in the ambush and had to be taken back to the Warlon home world where I was treated, I was later given this medal." Bob showed the medal to Lt. Braag.

Lt. Braag stood up, saluted Bob and stated, "That is the Warlon Medal of Honor and it is not given out lightly. I only know of one other then a Warlon who has ever received it . . . You are him . . . you are considered a warrior hero in the eyes of the Warlons and the whole of the Warlon Empire. Your name is on the great wall of Warriors."

Just then commander Reese entered the room and walked over to the table. "The captain wishes to see you at once Mr. Larson," he stated.

Then the three of them left the lounge and headed for the bridge. When they got there captain Pierce was already in his ready room. Lt. Braag took his station and commander Reese escorted Bob in to see the captain.

"Captain Larson," Pierce said when they entered. "Please sit. It seems a member of my crew saw fit to transport over to your ship without permission. We have been unable to establish contact with her for a few minutes now."

"She?" Larson asked.

"Yes," replied captain Pierce.

"Is this woman the Berillion we talked about earlier?" Bob asked once again. But before captain Pierce could reply there was a bright flash of light and Leah was standing in the room. "Leah!" Bob shouted. They grabbed each other and embraced for quite a while.

"I take it you know each other," Captain Pierce interrupted and stated.

"Yes," Bob and Leah both replied at the same time. "Leah is my wife she is Gheron's daughter," Bob said. "I thought I would spend an eternity looking for her. It was like trying to find a needle in a haystack."

"Yes. I understand," captain Pierce said as he turned to face Leah. "You never mentioned that you were married Leah."

"It has been a very long time since I have had any news about Bob," Leah said. "And I knew that I had to go on with my life."

"What do you intend to do now that you have found Leah?" Pierce asked Bob.

"I don't know," Bob replied. "If it's all the same to you, I would like to remain on board the Duncan for a little while just until other arrangements can be made in regards to Leah and myself. I don't know what her position is on this ship and I certainly do not want to cause her any trouble . . ."

"I can assure you captain Larson, you will not be causing her any trouble," captain Pierce interjected. "Leah is not in the Space fleet so she is free to go anywhere she likes, if she so chooses, and you are welcome to stay as long as you like, as well, captain Larson."

"Thank you captain Pierce, I appreciate that," Bob said. "I will go over to my . . . our ship and prepare her for the journey."

"About your ship?" Commander Reese asked. "May we have a look at it? We have no records of a ship like that in any of our data banks."

"Well, commander, it's really not up to me now. You see the ship technically still belongs to Leah so if it is all right with her, I would be glad to show you around," Bob replied.

"It's ok with me," Leah said. "Go ahead."

"Drop your shields 'Babe' we are going to have company over," Bob said.

"What did you just call your ship?" Reese asked.

"Babe. I call her Babe. I have been with the ship for so long that I have given her a nick—name," Bob said. "It helps when I have to do some quick communicating and since I have no crew I need not be so formal. Will you be joining us captain Pierce?"

"Maybe at a later time," Pierce replied. "Thank you though."

"Would it be ok to bring Lt. Commander Droid along?" Commander Reese asked.

"If it's ok with Leah, then it's ok with me," Bob said.

"It is fine with me," Leah said. Then Bob, Leah and Commander Reese exited, picked up Droid and headed for the Arrgott . . .

The captain was going over some reports on the PC when the door chime sounded. "Come in," he said. The door opened and councilor Meg Wauld entered. "Please sit councilor," Captain pierce said. "What can I do for you?"

"In the conference room earlier," Meg started. "I could not read captain Larson's thoughts or his emotions."

"Do you think he is hiding something councilor?" The captain asked.

"I don't think so," Meg continued. "As a trained psychologist I did not see anything in captain Larson's posture or attitude that would indicate hostility or danger. He must have a very controlled mind, to have been able to survive for over three hundred years in space and do it alone. That is no small task."

"True," Pierce replied. "But maybe his developed telepathic ability with his ship has enabled him to block out any unauthorized attempts to read his thoughts."

"I don't think so," Meg said. "To be able to block out all forms of thought would take a lot of concentration and skill. And even as he was relating his story to us his guard did not waiver one bit."

"Do you think he could be getting help from his ship?" Pierce asked. "Or, perhaps the ship itself could be providing the block."

"That certainly could be a possibility. We know very little about this living ship," Meg replied. "Perhaps the Berillions encountered this ship-like creature and discovered that it allowed humanoid beings to use them as if they were a space ship. For whatever reason that is unclear to us maybe they need to have this ship to humanoid contact."

"Ok then," Pierce said. "For whatever reason we must respect captain Larson's privacy, until he chooses otherwise. Perhaps in time when he feels more relaxed he will let down his guard a bit. I want you to talk to him, become his friend, right now he is a stranger to our time and his only familiar is Leah and his ship. He will need some friends."

"Yes captain. I'll drop by and see him after he returns," Meg stated and then she got up and left . . .

Over on the Arrgott Droid, Reese, Leah and Bob were talking and touring the leviathan. Bob showed everyone the Cryo chamber. Droid studied a control panel.

"Many centuries before I even met them, the Berillions' had turned from violence and war and concentrated on peace, medicine, science and the arts," Bob explained as they went along. "They were able to build perhaps the most advanced society of all . . ."

"Forgive the interruption but what does this station do?" Droid asked.

"This is the ships interface with the Cryo chamber," Bob answered. "With this I am able to receive information while I am in the chamber. The ship can give me information, on a subconscious level, and keep me up to date with what is going on around it. It's something I learned from my era, our doctors discovered, quite by accident, that our subconscious can be used to help people learn and understand information much quicker and with more detail then the conventional way of learning."

"I can use a very similar technique with the computers on the Duncan," Droid offered.

"Is this ship a fair example of the other ships used by your people Leah?" commander Reese asked.

"This ship might have a few more amenities built into it because it was mine, but for the most part it is a pretty standard setup," Leah answered.

After touring the rest of the ship Droid and Reese thanked them and beamed back the Duncan to let them finish getting the ship ready for docking and towing. When they were back on board the Duncan commander Reese and Lt. commander Droid reported back to the bridge.

"How was the tour?" Pierce asked.

"Impressive," commander Reese said. "All of the mechanical systems that Mr. Larson added seem to mesh right in with rest of the entities interior. You can hardly tell that it didn't belong there. You must get over and see it for yourself."

"I will arrange a trip later but for now I will just look over your report instead," captain Pierce said. "Set a course for the nearest star base."

"Course plotted and laid in sir," the helmsman said. "Star base one five one."

"When captain Larson and Leah return we'll head out," Pierce said.

Chapter Ten

Over on the Arrgott, Bob and Leah were finishing up and preparing to beam back over to the Duncan. As they worked they were discussing what they would do next, now that they had found each other.

"I'm a little nervous about where we will go," Bob said.

"Now's not the time to dwell on the subject," Leah said. "We will figure things out in due time. We have to hurry and get back."

"I must get something from my cabin for the captain," Bob said. He entered the cabin and came back out with a bottle of brandy for captain Pierce. "Captain Pierce should like this," Bob said. Now they were ready to go.

They called the Duncan and asked to be beamed over. That next day, Robert was being shown around the Duncan by a crew member when they meet up with the ships councilor, Meg.

"How are you getting along?" she asked.

"Fine," Bob answered. "Everything is so fantastic, our society has sure come a long way in the last three hundred years."

"Yes, it has," Meg stated. "But it hasn't always been easy. There has been more than a few minor altercations with some difficult races. But we have managed to overcome most of those obstacles. Where were you taking him?" she asked the crew member.

"We were going to sickbay," the crew member replied.

"I'll take over from here," Meg said. "You can report back to your section. So, captain Larson . . ."

"Please, councilor, call me Bob," he interjected.

"All right then you can call me Meg. So, Bob, how are you feeling?" she asked.

"Ah, trying to analyze the old pea huh? Trying to see if I've lost any marbles over the years?" Bob asked as he took her arm.

"Well, is it that obvious?" Meg replied.

"I can understand your concerns Meg," Bob said. "You are an empathic; and it must be a little disconcerting for you to not be able to read into my thoughts."

"A little bit, so how do you do it?" Meg asked.

"It's not me. I'm not doing anything," Bob said. "It's Babe and she is only trying to protect me. We have been together for over three hundred years and we have bonded . . ."

"Bonded? What do you mean?" Meg asked.

"It's nothing weird or anything like that," Bob explained. "It's just that we have this telepathic connection and it's very strong now. It took a very long time for Babe and I to achieve it, after all, I'm only human. I can't pretend to understand the scope of her abilities either. I've only come to accept them. I believe Babe is protecting me as I would protect her. She doesn't want to see me get hurt."

"Do you think she loves you?" Meg asks.

"Ah, clever Meg, no I don't think its love. I believe it's just a deep feeling of mutual respect for one another. So, how'd I do?" Bob asked.

"It's obvious to me that you are extremely well balanced," Meg said and then laughed. "You do not appear to be suffering any problems."

Bob stopped for just a second, turned, faced Meg and winked.

"Whoa! What was that?" Meg gasped. She was suddenly bombarded with overwhelming feelings of emotion.

Meg was shaking and Bob had both of his hands on her shoulders holding her steady. Then just as quickly as it started, it stopped. Meg looked up at Bob and all she did was just nodded for a moment. "I understand now," she stated. "Thank you for showing me that."

"Not a problem Meg. I thought maybe I owed you a little more than just a blank slate to stare at," Bob replied. "Now you have a little something to put in your report to the captain."

Meg laughed, and they continued talking as they walked to sickbay . . .

Later, in sickbay doctor Balow was giving Bob a medical examination.

"Well Dr. Balow, am I going to live"? Bob asked.

"All tests are excellent," she replied. "You are healthy as can be captain Larson and please, call me Ann."

"Thank you, Ann, and you can call me Bob," he added.

"Ok," Ann said and then asked. "I can't believe you haven't suffered any ill effects from prolonged bouts in your Cryo chamber, how do you do it?"

"Two weeks prior to going into stasis," Bob explained. "I change my diet, build up my immune system with vitamins, minerals and exercise and then I purge as many toxins from my body as I can . . ."

Just then Droid entered the room. "I am sorry to interrupt doctor," Droid stated. "The captain wishes to see Mr. Larson. Are you finished with your examination?"

"Yes we're finished and Bob is good to go," Dr. Balow said.

"Thank you doctor," Droid said and then he escorted Bob out of sickbay and headed for the bridge. "Captain Larson . . ." Droid started when Bob interrupted him.

"Droid, you don't have to call me captain call me Bob instead," Bob said.

"Ok," Droid continued. "As you wish . . . Bob. I would like to ask you a question."

"Go on," Bob replied.

"I do not fully understand how it is you learn while you sleep, could you explain it to me?" Droid asked.

"In the mid twentieth century, scientists discovered the power of subliminal suggestion," Bob said. "It was discovered that people could retain information when they listened to it repeatedly often while they slept. They realized that people were learning on a subconscious level. Back then, our doctors and scientists were only just beginning to understand the human minds capabilities. Some scientists used this knowledge to help people overcome obstacles, others used it as a way to get rich. Soon there were all sorts of self-help audiotapes for sale to the people. And so with the help of my ship, I was able to adapt this technology into my Cryo chamber and that is how I use it to learn alien languages and customs."

They arrived at the end of the corridor and entered the turbo lift for the bridge.

"I can plug into the ships computer by using fiber optic cables hooked into my neural network in my positronic matrix," Droid said. "I believe it must be very similar."

The turbo lift stopped at the bridge and the two exited.

Captain Pierce greeted captain Larson then asked, "Mr. Larson, I trust you are comfortable?"

"Yes I am. Thank you captain Pierce," Bob replied.

Captain Pierce then asked Bob to join him in his ready room so they could talk. Inside the ready room captain Pierce asked Bob to sit. Captain Pierce thanked Bob for the brandy.

"Do you have any plans yet for the future now that you've found Leah?" Captain Pierce asked.

"Not really," Bob answered. "I've been asking myself what could I do but I am at a loss."

"Well," the captain started. "The League of United Planets could use you as a historian. You see there are parts of Earth's history that are missing or unclear in our records. You could fill in some of the gaps if you are interested."

"I never thought that I'd be called a historian," Bob replied. "I don't know how much I could help."

"It's unimportant now," The captain said. "The main thing is to get you settled in somewhere. After we get to star base one five one maybe you can go back to Earth and take up residence again."

"That would be nice," Bob said. "But I don't even know if my property still exists. Besides, I've kind of gotten used to traveling around and it might be hard for me to settle back down again."

"I will check into it for you," the captain told him. "I'm sure though, that whatever you decide you want to do, the League of United Planets would not mind."

"Thank you. How long would it be before we reached this star base one five one?" Bob asked.

"We'll be there in six days," Pierce said. "Relax and take advantage of what the Duncan has to offer."

"Thank you captain," Bob said.

"I will." When they had finished their talk they got up and walked out of the ready room and over to the turbo lift doors. "If you should want to talk some more just holler," Bob said as he entered the lift.

"I'll do that, Mr. Larson," Pierce said as the doors closed.

One day Bob was in the holo deck working out with one of Lt. Braag's combat programs when the door opened and Lt. Braag walked in.

"Computer freeze program," Bob said. "I apologize Lt. Braag for using one of your programs without asking, but I have to keep in shape somehow."

"That is ok sir," Lt. Braag said. "The programs are here for anyone to use. What level are you on?"

"I'm on level four," Bob said. "For reasons unknown to me the computer won't let me go any higher."

"I am shocked the computer even allowed it," Lt. Braag said. "That's high for non Warlons."

"It was difficult to convince the computer as well," Bob said. "But after clearing the first and second levels, twice, the computer finally allowed me to advance to level three and now finally to level four. I will leave and get cleaned up so that you can work out without distraction."

"I would be honored if you stay and work out with me," Lt. Braag said. "After all, it isn't every day I get to fight next to a hero."

"Thanks, Lt.," Bob said. "I'm honored by your invitation." Bob ordered the computer to reset and start over with level two and then they started their work out together . . .

That evening Bob and Leah were in her quarters and Bob asked her if she could help him locate any living relatives of his, mainly, he wanted to know if his daughter had any children.

"That is not a problem at all," Leah said. "I only need to know your children's full names, dates and places of birth.

"I only had one daughter," Bob replied. "Her name was Angelica Mae Larson. She was born July eighteenth nineteen eighty-three in Lake city, Minnesota."

Leah input the information into the computer and in about a minute the results were displayed on the screen. She started to read it. "Angelica, married June twentieth, two thousand ten. She had three children . . ."

"Forward to present," Bob interrupted.

She scrolled down and continued reading, "Here we are, three descendants, two female and one male. Two are living on Earth and the other is currently in Space fleet, serving on the science vessel Viceroy."

Bob was pleased and then he made arrangements to contact each of them and let them know what was going on. "I hope they want to see me," he said.

"I'm sure they would appreciate that and I'm pretty sure they would not turn down your offer to meet with them," Leah offered. She turned down the lights and suggested that they get some sleep. The next day Bob gave captain Pierce a tour of the Arrgott. They had arrived at the Cryo chamber.

"This is quite a setup," Pierce said. "How does it work?"

"Well," Bob started. "After I have completed all of my preparations, I enter the pod. I would then be placed into a very deep sleep, and then the pod would be filled with a special liquid that is hyper oxygenated. The temperature would be lowered to three degrees Celsius."

"Are there any ill effects?" Pierce asked.

"None so far," Bob answered. "The liquid in the pod protects my body from any freeze damage that might occur should the temperature accidentally fall below the freezing point. That is how I am able to survive repeated stasis cycles." Then the captain asked to see the bridge so Bob led him down a long corridor and they came to a door.

The door opened they entered onto the bridge. The bridge was circular, about seven meters in diameter, and in the center was a single contoured, reclining chair.

"Is this the command chair?" Pierce asked.

"Yes it is," Bob replied with a smile. "I do sit here sometimes but it is not necessary for me to even be on the bridge at all times. You see, I am constantly in contact with the ship and her sensors telepathically. I can command from anywhere onboard, even from inside the Cryo chamber itself."

"How is that possible?" Pierce asked. "You said you are in a state of suspended animation!"

"Although I am sleeping," Bob explained. "I am plugged in to the ships systems on a subconscious level. My mind becomes an extension of the ship, all information is routed to my subconscious mind, and in a way, I become like a secondary computer and help determine strategies and, with the ships own intelligence as a guide, decisions are made and orders are executed. And in the case of a major emergency the ship will follow a predetermined set of orders, bring me out of stasis, and protect itself and me until I am fully in control to deal with the situation. But more important, the leviathan actually does not need any input from me to function at all, as it is alive and therefore able to travel through space on its own."

"Amazing, truly remarkable!" Pierce exclaimed.

They continued to tour the ship for another thirty minutes and then they returned to the Duncan. Back on the Duncan captain Pierce was on the bridge and Reese asked him how he liked the tour, the captain told him that it was a very interesting tour and that the leviathan was truly an amazing creature.

Droid informed the captain that they would be at star base one five one in two hours, forty-seven minutes and thirty-eight seconds. Pierce thanked him for the report as he headed for his ready room.

"You have the bridge commander Reese," Pierce said as left the bridge.

Chapter Eleven

In the Duncan's lounge, Bob and Leah were talking. "We will be at the star base in three hours or so, what will you do then?" She asked.

"Don't you mean what we will do? You are coming with me aren't you?" Bob asked.

"I don't think I could leave the Duncan at this time," Leah answered. "You can take the Arrgott and continue using her for as long as you want. Now that you know how to reach me we can see each other whenever we want to." Bob knew that when Leah said something like that, he could trust that there was a good reason for her wanting to stay and he did not argue the point any more.

"After all these years of separation I did not realize how hard it would be to just start right back up as if nothing had changed," Bob said.

"I agree," Leah said. "If you want to we can retake our marriage vows."

Bob was somewhat surprised by her statement. "Is that what you really want to do?" Bob asked. "Please be honest with me."

"It would be hard to pretend that the past three hundred years or so didn't happen," Leah said. "But they did. I have made a lot of friends since the destruction of my world and it would be hard to give that up."

"Well, we don't have to get remarried," Bob said. "We can continue on, now that we know how to contact each other."

Leah agreed and they embraced and kissed, just then the ships alarm sounded for yellow alert. Back on the bridge Lt. Braag informed the captain that the ships sensors had detected some strange energy readings up ahead.

"Take us out of light speed," Pierce barked. "Go to one half speed! Droid, report!"

"Scans indicate a high concentration of neutrino particles mixed inside a plasma cloud one hundred thousand kilometers wide by two hundred thousand kilometers long sir. If we come in contact with the neutrino filled plasma cloud we could sustain severe damage to the ship and crew even with our shields at maximum," Droid reported. Pierce ordered the ship to a full stop. "The plasma cloud appears to be on a direct course that will take it in contact with star base one five one," Droid reported. "If that were to happen it would cause a reaction in the atmosphere that could destroy a significant amount of life on the planet sir."

The captain ordered all findings be sent to the star base and that they should prepare to evacuate as soon as possible.

"I sense a basic instinct level intelligence coming from the cloud captain," counselor Wauld reported.

"Let's try and communicate with it. Bring the universal translator on line," the captain ordered.

He tried to hail the plasma cloud but there was no response. Then the cloud started to slow its speed.

"I am sensing confusion and agitation now captain," Meg offered. The turbo lift doors opened and Robert and Leah entered the bridge. Bob saw the cloud on the view screen and told the captain that it was krill. The captain looked at Mr. Larson and asked him to explain what he meant.

"I have had contact with this matter before," Bob explained. "I have dubbed it krill because the Arrgott feeds on this matter like a whale back on Earth feeds on krill. Could you move the Duncan about one million kilometers out from here?"

"Yes," replied the captain. "What do you have in mind?"

"Trust me," Bob continued. "Do you have about ten thousand cubic feet of cargo space for my equipment from the Arrgott?"

"There is room in cargo bay four captain," Lt. Braag offered as he studied his console.

With the captain's permission Lt. Braag sent the coordinates to the Arrgott. The Arrgott transported the equipment to the Duncan's cargo hold and then detached itself.

"Go feed Babe," Bob said as she flew away.

The bridge crew watched as the leviathan fed on the plasma cloud.

"How long do you think this will take?" captain Pierce asked after several minutes had passed.

"It has been a long time since there was this much krill for babe to feed on," Bob said. "Give her another fifteen minutes and then she will have a full belly."

With her belly full of fresh food Babe was feeling playful so Bob sent her off to burn up some energy but told her to be back in a couple of hours. Droid reported that the plasma cloud had been broken up and dissipated to a safe level and that it no longer posed a threat to the Duncan or the star base.

"Transmit the information to star base one five one and tell them they do not need to evacuate," Pierce ordered. "How much longer to the star base?"

"It will take two hours, ten minutes and twenty-seven seconds at light speed three sir," Droid reported.

"Thank you Mr. Droid. Proceed," Pierce said. "Will you join me in my quarters Mr. Larson?"

"Sure captain," Bob replied. "You have the bridge commander Reese," captain Pierce said as he left the bridge with Bob.

"What have you decided to do Mr. Larson?" Pierce asked when they got to his quarters.

"I have learned of three grandchildren," Bob said. "I have sent word to all of them to arrange a meeting. I'll probably keep on traveling and exploring after a brief rest though."

"Will Leah be going with you?" Pierce asked.

"Not for now but we will keep in touch," Bob answered. "I'll keep the ship and I'll come by and visit again you can be sure."

"I would enjoy that," Pierce said. "I will be looking forward to the visit." They chatted for a while and were having a drink when the intercom came to life.

"Commander Reese to Captain Pierce," the voice said. "We are now in orbit above star base one five one."

"Acknowledged," captain Pierce replied. "Well. I had better be getting back to the bridge, thank you again for the brandy and the opportunity to talk to you and get to know you a little better captain Larson."

"The pleasure is mine and please, just call me Bob, I'm not in the service captain Pierce," Robert stated.

"All right then," Pierce said. "And you can call me Jon."

"Thank you Jon for your hospitality," Bob said as he shook Jon's hand. "Would it be ok to say goodbye to some of the crew before I leave?"

"By all means," Jon said. "Go ahead and take your time we are going to be here for several days."

They both got up and walked out into the corridor, Jon going one direction and Bob another.

Chapter Twelve

Captain Pierce was sitting in his ready room going over requests for shore leave when lt. commander Driod informed him that there was a priority one call from the admiral of the Space fleet.

"I'll take it in here," captain Pierce replied . . .

After several minutes the captain entered onto the bridge, he seemed visibly shaken.

"What is wrong, captain," Meg asked.

"It seems that Mr. Larson is wanted by the authorities back on Earth," Pierce said. "I contacted the league, a while back, to find out some information for Mr. Larson. I just received word from admiral Anderson that he is to be returned at once."

"What has he done?" commander Reese asked.

"The admiral wouldn't say," captain Pierce said. "I was told just to see that he got there as soon as possible. Where is he now lt. Braag?"

"He is in the ships lounge," lt. Braag said.

"Your with me lt. Braag," he said as he got up. "You have the bridge commander."

In the ships lounge Bob and Leah were enjoying a meal and discussing what they were going to do next.

"You have to go and see the captain immediately," Bob told her suddenly.

"Why? What is wrong? Did you get a message from Babe?" She asked.

"Yes, and you have to go now," Bob told her. Leah got up and hesitated.

"Go. Now," Bob said.

Leah headed for the door and she looked back at Bob and he motioned for her to keep going. She stepped out into the corridor just as captain Pierce and Lt. Braag got there.

"Where is Mr. Larson," Pierce asked.

"He's inside," she answered. "What is going on? He just told me that I had to go see you."

Captain Pierce and lt. Braag entered the lounge with Leah on their heels.

"Hello Jon," Bob said. "I know why you came down here."

"Will someone tell me what is going on?" Leah asked. "The captain received a message from Space fleet," Bob

said. "It seems I'm supposed to be taken back to Earth." "Yes," Pierce said. "How did you know that?"

"Babe informed me," Bob said. "She picked up the transmission from Space fleet."

"She can do that?" Pierce asked.

"Yes," Leah said this time. "She can do a lot of things."

Leah telepathically asked Babe to beam her and Bob over but nothing happened.

'She won't do anything,' Bob thought to Leah. 'How come,' Leah thought back.

'Because I told her not to do anything for now,' Bob replied telepathically.

"Will you come with us?" Pierce asked.

"Yes. You will not have any trouble from me," Bob said.

"Jon, tell me what is going on," Leah said to Pierce.

"I don't know anything at this point," Jon told her. "I am in the dark here. I was only told to get him back to Earth fast."

The four of them left the lounge and went to the conference room so they could talk.

"What does Earth want from you Bob?" Pierce asked. "I don't know actually," Bob replied. "The last time I

was there was in two thousand and two I think. The year I left for good. I haven't been back since. And that is the truth."

"Well the League's High Council wants you there as soon as possible," Pierce said. "If we leave now we can be there in two weeks at top speed."

"Or we can be there in a little under ten days," Leah stated.

"How?" Bob and Pierce ask simultaneously.

"You don't know it Bob, but Babe can do some pretty amazing things. She can fly faster then any Space fleet vessel to date," Leah said.

"Just how fast are we talking?" Pierce asked.

"I'll just say it is well over two times the current top speed of the Duncan," Leah answered.

"I didn't know that," Bob said. "How come you never told me Babe?"

There was no response from Babe this time.

"You're not allowed to know everything Bob," Leah said. "Us girls have got to have our secrets. I can take Bob back to Earth quicker and you have my word that I will."

"I would like to come with," Pierce said. "That is if it is ok with you Leah."

"Jon doesn't trust you Leah," Bob said.

"There isn't anyone on this ship that I trust more then Leah," Jon said. "If she tells me she will take you to Earth, then I believe her, no questions. I just want to be there, in your corner, when we stand in front of the League High Council."

"It is ok with me Jon, when do you want to leave?" Leah said.

"We will leave in two hours," Jon said. "Sounds good," Leah said.

They all left to get ready for the trip. Captain Pierce was in his quarters packing for the trip, commander Reese was with him.

"Recall all shore leave and head for Earth at top speed," Pierce said. "Hopefully I will have some information as to what is going on by the time you get there."

"Let's just hope that it's some kind of misunderstanding," Reese said.

"Yes," Pierce said and with that he went to find Bob and Leah.

Bob and Leah were in her quarters packing for the trip.

"I sure wish I knew what this was all about," she said. "I am starting to get worried."

"It's no picnic for me either," Bob said. "I'm sure this is just a simple mistake that can be cleared up quickly."

"I hope so too," Leah said.

Leah and Bob had just left her quarters when captain Pierce arrived.

"We are ready Jon," Leah said.

Then they headed for the transporter room and beamed over to the Arrgott. Bob showed Jon to his cabin and told him that dinner would be ready in an hour and then he carried Leah's bags to their cabin. They spent the next several days discussing what Bob could have done to bring about his being called to Earth.

"Tell me everything that happened while you were home," Jon said.

"There's not much to tell really," Bob said. "There was this FBI agent that tried his darnedest to have me arrested. But I never gave him any ammo that he could use against me."

"Why was the FBI after you in the first place?" Jon asked.

"The only thing I can think of was back then the United States government had created laws that made it illegal to make contact with extraterrestrials," Bob said. "Which was kind of stupid because their standard policy was that there was no such thing as extraterrestrials. So when Gheron's ship crashed I hid it as soon as possible and then doctored the crash site to make it look like the government had already gotten there and cleaned it up."

"Why?" Jon asked.

"Because I, like many Americans, didn't trust the government," Bob continued. "I didn't want them getting their hands on those aliens and their ship. Sure it was against the law back then but surely not today? The statute of limitations should have long since expired by now."

"Maybe I can get admiral Anderson to tell me more about the reason they want you," Jon said.

"It is worth a chance," Leah said.

Captain Pierce went to his cabin to contact Admiral Anderson. He was only gone for about fifteen minutes and then he returned to Leah's cabin.

"Admiral Anderson couldn't give me any explanation," Jon said. "Either he doesn't know or he is under strict orders no to say."

"We should arrive at Earth in twelve hours," Leah offered. "It will be late in the evening when we arrive so we won't be able to find anything out for sure for at least eighteen hours. Until then we should adjust our time so that when we get there we will be rested and ready."

When the Arrgott was about two hours out from Earth orbit, two military escort ships pulled along side. Captain Pierce contacted them and told them that he was on board and that there would be no trouble. When they were in orbit a shuttle came up to transport them to the surface. When they arrived at the High Council Chamber, Jon and Leah were asked to sit in the back while Bob was escorted to the front and seated. The room was filled with delegates and civilians from all the known League worlds. Some races Bob recognized while others he did not.

An official entered the front of the room and asked everyone to rise. Seven robed figures entered and were seated at the Council table. After everyone was seated, the Chief Justice asked Robert to please stand and move forward.

"Please state your full name for the record," he said. "My name is Robert John Larson," Bob stated.

"Please state your date of birth and where you are from," was the next command.

"I was born on June sixth, nineteen hundred and fifty-nine and I am from Earth," he replied.

"Mr. Larson," one of the other justices said. "You have been charged by your government with treason. How do you respond?"

"What do you mean by treason?" Bob asked.

"You are charged with aiding extraterrestrial aliens and hiding their ship and then allowing them to escape without informing the leaders of your government," a third justice said.

"By government," Bob started. "Do you mean mine or yours?"

"It's one and the same," came the reply.

"I beg to differ," Bob said. "My government doesn't exist any more. It's been gone for over three hundred years now. A new and different one has replaced it and I have been told it is a much better one. How is it you can sit up there and accuse me of violating laws that do not exist anymore? Or at least, for the better, have been changed or abolished."

There was a slight murmur from the crowd.

"There will be order in this Council," the Chief justice said as he banged his gavel.

"I will tell you this Mr. Larson, there is no statute of limitations when it comes to treason," the Chief Justice told him.

"Then before I answer to any charges," Bob said. "I request legal council and time to prepare my defence."

"Granted. You will have one week to prepare and then you will be brought back here," the Chief Justice stated. "This Council will recess for one week."

Bob was escorted to the back of the hall and Leah and Jon joined him.

"Well played Bob," Jon said. "You bought yourself a week. Let's find you council and get started on your defence."

"I hope we can convince the League Council that this charge is invalid by today's laws," Leah said.

"You heard the Chief Justice," Bob said. "Supposedly there is no statute of limitations on treason. Back in my time a person could be put to death if convicted."

"We will see that it doesn't come to that," Jon said.

Then Bob, Leah and Jon were taken to their assigned quarters a few blocks down from the High Council Chambers. Jon made some calls to try and find a good attorney for Bob.

Chapter Thirteen

When Bob, Leah and Jon arrived at the High Council Chambers a week later, Bob was once again escorted to the front of the hall and seated; his attorney was already there. Jon and Leah were seated in the back. The chamber was filled to capacity; there was standing room only. It seemed that everyone wanted to be a part of the proceedings. The council was called to order and after the seven justices were seated they began.

"You have adequate council and have been given time to plan your defense," the Chief Justice said. "How do you answer the charges Mr. Larson?

"I plead not guilty," Bob answered. "I call for the dismissal of all charges under the Sixth Amendment to the constitution of the United States of America."

The crowd let out a collective gasp.

"Order," the Chief Justice called as he banged his gavel and then he quickly checked his computer terminal. He brought up the Sixth amendment and read it.

Amendment Six

In all criminal prosecutions, the accused shall enjoy the right to a speedy and public trial, by an impartial jury of the State and district wherein the crime shall have been committed, which district shall have been previously ascertained by law, and to be informed of the nature and cause of the accusation; to be confronted with the witnesses against him; to have compulsory process for obtaining witnesses in his favor, and to have the assistance of council for his defense' . . . From the Bill of Rights.

"I ask to see my accusers so that I might confront them," Bob said when the justices were finished reading.

"There are no witnesses," the Chief Justice said.

"Then by Constitutional law of The United States of America, I request that the charges against me be dropped," Bob said.

There is chatter from the crowd.

"Order, there will be order," the Chief said. "This council will recess for one hour."

Bob walked to the back of the hall and standing there was some of the crew of the Duncan; Tom, Meg, Ann, Droid and Braag.

"Hi guys," Bob said. "When did you get here?" "We got here just as the trial started," Tom said. "That was a clever opening," Jon said.

"It won't stall them for long," Bob said. "I'm sure they will come up with something. I've got to come up with something also. I can't believe this could be happening. At least not in this time period."

When the Council reconvened, the evidence against Bob was displayed on the view screen.

"Objection," Bob's attorney stated. "This evidence is all conjecture. Where is the actual proof that Mr. Larson has done any of the alleged crimes?"

"We have that right here," the Chief Justice stated and with that they displayed signed affidavits from some of the Berillions that Bob had helped.

"That evidence is inadmissible," Bob stated. "It is dated one hundred years after the fact. You can't use it. It wasn't collected during the time period when the alleged crime took place. Therefore I must protest."

"Any evidence collected during the investigation can be used in court," the Chief Justice stated. "Do you have any evidence to present in your defence?"

Just then the doors to the High Council chamber opened and three figures wearing long robes with hoods drawn over their heads walked in.

"Your Honor, may we approach the bench?" the lead figure asked.

"You may," the Chief Justice said.

"Thank you," he said and then he pulled his hood back.

All Bob could do was stand there and stare. He could not believe what he was seeing. It was Gheron, a slightly older version then the one he remembered, but Gheron nonetheless.

"How can this be?" Bob asked.

"It is good to see you my son," he said. "Our species is long lived and when I heard that you were in trouble I had to come."

Bob sat down.

"Your honor," Gheron started. "I would like to speak on Mr. Larson's behalf."

"I consider this an honor, Ambassador Gheron," the Chief Justice said. "Please continue."

"You have before you the creator of the great League of United Planets," Gheron said.

"We all know of your accomplishments Ambassador," the Chief Justice stated.

"I am not referring to myself," Gheron continued. "I was only the instrument through which the League prospered and grew. Sitting in this court today is the true creator of the League. It was his great inspiration that enabled me to start the journey. Without his vision, there would be no League of United Planets. Your honors and distinguished representatives, I give you the founder of the League of United Planets, Mr. Robert J. Larson."

There was a collective gasp and then the room fell silent.

"Impossible Ambassador Gheron," the Chief Justice said. "Everyone here knows that you started the League three hundred years . . . ago . . . Oh, ah please continue."

"Thank you your honor," Gheron said as he continued his testimony. "It is true that I went to the first ten planets on the initial charter personally and proposed that we join together. It took over ten years of talks but I managed to secure their pledge and so, the League of United Planets started. And now, three hundred years later, it has grown into the great League we have today. A League that consists of over ten thousand worlds and systems including Earth."

"How am I responsible?" Bob asked.

"Do you remember the conversation we had on Pogh, before you left?" Gheron asked him.

"Yes I do," Bob answered.

"That conversation inspired me," Gheron continued. "While we were talking Robert said something very profound. He told me of the old United Nations of Earth. He pondered about it and said that it was too bad that the civilized worlds throughout our sector weren't "United". He said that maybe if they were then the destruction of Berillion might have been avoided. He said that if the systems had been allied with each other then they might have collectively fought and repelled the Cyborg attack saving countless billions of lives. I was touched, such wisdom from a human from such a primitive planet . . ."

"Hey," Bob said.

"Sorry," Gheron said. "You know what I mean." "Yes," Bob said.

"It was a long and difficult mission but one that I was compelled to see through," Gheron said. "One fraught with danger and many perils along the way. But I never gave up, I had hope in my heart. I believed it could be done. Every day we have more and more systems asking to join and we grow stronger with every new addition. The quadrant is safer and better for it. But I am not the only one here that has something to say on Robert's behalf. If I may, I would like to ask that you listen to my friends who stand with me."

"Of course we will," the Chief Justice said.

Gheron sat down next to his old friend, and son in law Bob, at the defence table and then the second hooded figure stepped up and pulled his hood down. Bob studied the being, he recognized him as a Warlon but that was all for now.

"You don't recognize me do you old friend?" he asked Bob.

"Not at the moment," Bob replied.

"How is your shoulder brother?" He asked. Bob felt his shoulder then . . .

"Ktaal, is it really you?" Bob exclaimed, his eyes widening.

"Yes it is old friend," he replied and then he turned to the Justices. "I would just like to say that the Warlon Empire would not have joined the League when they did had it not been for my friend and brother Mr. Larson. Our two factions could very well still be fighting if it weren't for what he had done some fifty years ago. It was then that we met, in a cantina on Cantoo, and I was intent on killing him, but he bested my second and me in a fight that day. He either showed great courage or stupidity that day, but in the end we were the ones beaten and he was on top. He was allowed to come to the Warlon home world as my brother. No one dared mess with him and then one day word came to us that one of our outposts had been attacked near the Andromidan border."

"We sent ships and this young foolish human followed along. He proved himself well and helped us defeat the Andromidan attackers but not before getting himself injured while saving my life. He nearly died, so we took him back to Warlon and nursed him back to health. The Warlon Emperor himself presented him with the Warlon Medal of Honor in the Great Council hall. His image and story of courage hangs on the wall of Warriors. When Ambassador Gheron came to our world and talked of peace we were skeptical. Several years later he was back and still talking alliance. He was walking through the hall of the Great Council with the Emperor when he chanced upon the wall of Warriors. He stopped, looked at the picture and read the inscription. The Emperor told him the story about this human from Earth and then Ambassador Gheron told him that this human from Earth was his son in law."

"It was after hearing this that the Emperor realized, that if this human was willing to die for a people he didn't even know, a people that probably would have killed him on the spot had he strayed across their border, there just might be something to this alliance. A few years later, in the Great Council hall, the Warlons officially became members of the League of United Planets. I was chosen as their Ambassador because they credited me with bringing this human to them. Our races have enjoyed fifty years of peace, it would be a shame to tear that apart. My testimony is finished, let the last man have his say."

Ktaal sat next to Gheron at the defence table and the third alien stepped forward. When he pulled his hood back Bob nearly fainted on the spot. The man walked up to Bob and stuck out his hand.

"Hello my old friend," he said.

Bob was still shaking. He couldn't believe what his eyes were seeing. Through tear filled eyes he looked once more on the face of a friend he knew all to well to be long dead. But standing there, in front of him was his dearest friend from home, Bill.

"How can this be possible?" Bob cried.

Then Bill told Bob the secret he had kept all those years back on Earth long ago.

"I am from the planet Vergon," Bill explained. "We have been keeping an eye on Earth for centuries long before the Berillions."

Then he turned to the Justices and asked to speak. "By all means, please do," the Chief Justice said.

"Thank you," Bill said. "It is good to be back on Earth although I wish it could have been under nicer circumstances. I consider this planet to be my second home and I have known Mr. Larson for a very long time now. When I first met him on Earth I had a feeling that he would do something good. I sensed in him a compassion for humanity far stronger then in anyone else. If you are to find my friend guilty of this charge then you are going to have to find me guilty as well."

The crowd gasped collectively. No Vergon has ever been accused of any crime, ever.

"Yes," Bill continued when the crowd settled. "It was not by mere chance that I was the one who came out to investigate the scene when Gheron's small reconnaissance vessel came down. It was my duty to see that his ship and crew were not discovered. When I arrived at the location of the crash I was almost relieved that it had gone down where it did. Bob . . . sorry, I mean, Mr. Larson was so calm when he answered his door that night, I almost thought that he actually did not know what had happened there. When he offered to come out to the site with me I became suspicious. When we got to the site and I saw the elaborate lengths that he had gone through to keep me from finding the ship I decided to let it play out. He was very convincing when he tried to make me believe that men from the government had already been there and that they had carted the wreckage and bodies away. The shell casings were a nice touch by the way."

"Thanks Bill," Bob said. "I was hoping it would work."

"I know," Bill said and then he turned back to the judges. "So I decided to trust the instincts I had about Robert and I left. I secretly watched as he helped the Berillions with their ship and with Gheron and when the rescue ship came and went, I was relieved. Robert never once let on about what happened that night. And then a year later another ship came, only this one did not crash. When it left with Robert, I took care of his property and told everybody that he had gone on an extended vacation so that they would not be worried about him."

"When he returned a year and a half later he was different and there were a few new strangers in town. I knew who they were and I trusted Robert enough to let him keep doing what it was he was doing. I tried to protect him the best I could but finally his actions attracted the attention of the FBI. Robert was so calm when the FBI agent came to talk to him I knew he could handle himself. He was so good that when he actually told the agent that he had a space ship he didn't believe him. One thing led to another and over the next few years he would transport Berillion refugees off Earth but he always came home. Then one day he was gone and he did not return. I stayed on Earth for many years after that until it was time for me to return to Vergon."

"When Gheron came to Vergon with this plan to unite the systems in our sector I questioned him and he told me about my old friend, Robert. I told Gheron about him as well and he just said that it sure did sound like him. A lot of the credit for the charter worlds signing on goes to Robert. His willingness to put himself out there for races of people that would not otherwise give him the time of day, carried a lot of weight. It got them to thinking, if this one man, a human, was willing to take a risk, then far be it for them to dismiss it completely."

"Does anyone here, know the names of the planets listed on the original League Charter? I am not talking about the copies in the files. I am talking about the very first original draft. Well I have it here. Ambassador Gheron brought it to Vergon for safekeeping. You all may think you know the names of the original planets and that there were only ten of them. Well I am here to tell you that there were eleven planets."

With that Ambassador William Mont from Vergon displayed the original charter on the view screens in the Council chambers. The Justices read it, the crowd read it, and everyone was awestruck. For there, the first name at the very top of the list was: Robert John Larson, Earth. The crowd in the Council chambers went wild, the clapping and cheering went on for ten minutes. After the crowd settled down the Chief Justice restored order and then, after talking it over with the other six Justices, he gave their ruling.

"We, the League of Council, do hereby order that all charges against Mr. Robert J. Larson be dropped and that no action be taken against him or his assigns. Case dismissed."

Leah and the crew of the Duncan came forward to congratulate Bob. People were cheering, tears were flowing. There was a celebration being planned. Bob met his grand children. A few days later Bob was back in Minnesota on the farm; it seemed that one of his grand daughters had inherited it. He had planned a small gathering for his friends and newfound family. The command crew of the Duncan was there; Jon, Tom, Ann, Meg, Braag and Droid. Gheron was there along with Dahl. Ktaal was there but most importantly, his best and dearest friend, Bill was there.

Bob noticed that everyone seemed to be having a good time except Bill, who was off to one side just hanging on the fringe.

Bob strolled over and said, "Hey Bill, how ya doin?" "Fine Bob," Bill said. "Thanks."

"Man, I never thought in a Berillion years that I would ever see you again," Bob said.

"Good one Bob," Bill said. "I try," Bob said.

"I am sorry that I could not tell you about me back then," Bill said. "Our non interference policy."

"That's cool," Bob said. "And all those times I kept telling folks about "our" ship. Man I bet you wanted to smack the shit outta me?"

"You know," Bill said as a smile appeared on his face. "That was actually kind of funny. We had our own running gag and no one was the wiser. Thank you Bob."

"For what?" Bob asked.

"For being the man that you were . . . are," Bill said. "The man with the plan." Bob said.

"No. The man with the grand plan," Bill corrected. "Thanks Bill. Hey don't be such a wallflower, come on

let's go meet these guys," Bob said.

Bob introduced the crew of the Duncan to his old friend Bill. They were all standing at perfect attention.

"What's up with that Bill?" Bob asked.

"I guess they don't know me like you do Bob," he replied.

"Hey guys," Bob said. "This is Bill, you know; the sheriff deputy, my best friend from here, Minnesota."

"Yes, quite true," captain Pierce said. "But he is also the Ambassador from Vergon. We rarely get to meet a member of one of the League's oldest and wisest races."

"Man you sure got them fooled," Bob whispered. "Shush," Bill said and then laughed that all to familiar laugh that Bob thought he would never hear again.

75

The End.